UR-image

UR-image

JOHN C. WOODCOCK

iUniverse, Inc.
Bloomington

UR-image

PERMISSIONS:
Cover: abstract swirling vortex © L. Shat and Newgrange © Tetastock: Fotolia.com.
Interior: all graphics are the author's

iUniverse books may be ordered through booksellers or by contacting:

iUniverse
1663 Liberty Drive
Bloomington, IN 47403
www.iuniverse.com
1-800-Authors (1-800-288-4677)

ISBN: 978-1-4759-9690-6 (sc)
ISBN: 978-1-4759-9691-3 (ebk)

Printed in the United States of America

iUniverse rev. date: 06/27/2013

ACKNOWLEDGMENTS

For texts not cited in the interior:

1991: GARY: Epigram is by the author; poem is by author; quoted passage from Goethe's *Faust* is in public domain.

1999: ALLEN: Poem is by author.

1965: THE RETURN AND ON: Quotes and poem by author.

2025: ALLEN'S BOOK OF QUOTATIONS: Quotes in order: Parmenides; Rodriguez, A.; Lawrence, D. H.; Hillman, J.; Rilke, M.; inuit shaman (anonymous); Barfield, O.; Yeats, W. B.; Jung, C. G.; Graves, R.; Graves, R.; Benét, S. V.; Cohen, L.; Barfield, O.; Eco, U.; Barfield, O.; Rowling, J. K.; Jamison, K. R.; Lockhart, R. A.; Steiner, R.

2013: THE VOICE OF PO': Poems by author.

AUTHOR'S FOREWORD

I HAVE BEEN WRITING FOR twenty-five years or so. I have written nine books now, many articles and essays, and poetry. I have also created some works of art. I keep a dream journal and have countless note books. I have also completed a master's degree and doctoral degree, both of which required years of putting pen to paper, or finger to keyboard.

Only in my academic writing did I receive some formal training but I still do not know how to type beyond the two-fingered method. In all my other literary output, I received no training or coaching in the craft of writing. I simply do not conceive of my life as being that of an author. I do not consider the craft of writing as a career for me. I apparently picked up what I needed in order to say what I wanted to say, as I went along. When, finally, some kind individuals agreed to edit a small piece or two, I was shocked at the degree to which their careful editing exposed holes in my knowledge of grammar, spelling, punctuation, structural convention, formatting styles, etc.

Why then do I write at all?

One reason to write of course is to show others that you know what they know, i.e. to communicate your intellectual readiness to enter a community which is dedicated to a particular discipline. In this kind of writing, the personality of the author is not a topic. Instead, the writer must rise up to the level of the "theoretical 'I'" that is, the voice of the discipline itself. Personal opinions or feelings are not wanted here. This intellectual demand is well captured in the requirement that the author write in the 3rd person or with the "I" of the discipline and to produce citations wherever epistemological claims are made. The granting of a degree is the public sign that the individual has reached the intellectual standards set by the discipline.

Another reason to write concerns the craft of writing. An author may spend years developing and refining her craft, excelling at a genre for example. The author's personality remains relevant here in the sense that we, the readers, can recognize the signature of the literary work. For example, Isaac Asimov's signature, within the genre of Science Fiction novels, is readily discernible.

But there is yet another reason to write, one that has nothing to do with access to a body of knowledge or allegiance to an art form or genre of literature. I came across a vivid example of this "reason to write" recently in a movie, *Quills* (2000), which in part concerns the penmanship of the Marquis de Sade (Geoffrey Rush). He is imprisoned in an attempt to control his literary output but pen and ink are smuggled in; when these are removed, de Sade uses wine and blood as ink; when these are denied, he uses his own shit to smear words on walls etc. We can see from this example that another reason to write is because one is compelled to, with no regard for conventions, established genres, or anything else for that matter. The writer is seized!

I write because something is happening to me that forces me to write. My body heats up in an inflammatory reaction that can only be quenched, at least partially, by writing a process going on "within"—not writing *about* a process going on "within" but *writing* it as it is happening. My early books express this process in detail and I was too immersed in it to ask the question, "What am I doing?"; "What kind of writing is this?"; "Is it a genre of writing, or at least the beginnings of one?" I simply wrote. The fact that I could eventually ask this question, however, is a signal that, to some extent, the process was becoming conscious of itself and thus reflective. One of my early attempts to conceptualize the kind of writing I was doing appears this way: [1]

> I begin by paying attention to certain events occurring in the world: i.e. events characterized by qualities of the unusual, the unfamiliar, the startling, all of which obviously involve my psychological participation, and then I open myself up to these phenomena sufficiently for them to penetrate my consciousness, so that I begin to think the thought of the phenomenon, distinct from my thinking about them This process is in effect an initiation into another form of consciousness, the consciousness of the phenomenon. This finally can form the basis for new action in the world, action that is not simply a repeat of the known past but instead carries the germ of a new future. These actions always took me away from the security of the familiar into the unknown future.

> My method of writing is therefore an attempt to develop an art form that can demonstrate this process. I soften the boundaries of my ego and pay attention to unusual, unfamiliar, or even startling, images that "arrive". I take up a relationship with these visitors and am prepared to leave my present path to follow their hints. I record this process as it goes on. A kind of wandering therefore takes place in my writing, as in my life . . .

---

[1] Woodcock, J. C. (2012). *Living in Uncertainty Living with Spirit.* Bloomington. iUniverse. P. 77.

In this way, I move from a memory, to a dream, to a reflection of an event in the world, to an etymological study of a word, to the words of another author. I do not concern myself with any separation between inner and outer, past and future, fact and fiction i.e. the usual categories of experience. The one constant is that all my writing springs out of the soil of immediate experience and so is real. I pay attention to detail, or hints that emerge freely from "within", no matter how small or seemingly insignificant. It takes a kind of surrender to psychic process in order to write this way, and a faith that I won't fall merely into chaos, or madness. But this is far from certain!

This conception helped as I began to understand that the nature of my writing involved, not any genre or established craft, but a breakdown of such categories, and indeed, a breakdown of fundamental categories such as mechanical space and linear past, present, and future, those very categories that constitute the background of our stabilized modern structure of consciousness. This early formulation distinguishes what I had believed was merely a personal breakdown from an objective breakdown of categories occurring "in the background" of modern consciousness. This real process at present has no category with which to name and therefore grasp it, since it involves a *breakdown* in categories. I could use names like "fictive", or "imaginative", but these categories come loaded with a history that has deprived them of any truth or reality. In fact these words currently mean the opposite—not real, fantasy, entertainment only, falsity, etc.

But the phenomenology is conclusive. This process is real and has no referent outside itself. For example a breakdown of categories does not refer outside itself to a literal break down on a personal level or to the scale of a literal world catastrophe, although many people who are caught up in these background movements often make these misinterpretations. And yet, because this movement is the real background or the "within-ness" of the world, then it follows that madness or world catastrophe are not to be excluded after all.

How can we understand the necessity of this contradiction?

An example may help us here. C. G. Jung had a series of "world catastrophe" visions just prior to the outbreak of the First World War. In his book *Memories, Dreams, Reflections* he offers two contradictory interpretations. [2] Being an experienced psychiatrist he understood psychosis very well and at first felt he was being menaced by one. But when the war broke out he began wonder instead how his personal inner experiences could have something to do with subsequent events in the real world (the catastrophe of the war). This question of the connection between inner psychic events and outer events in the world became a lifetime's work for Jung, and is no less important and perhaps no more understood today.

For the next several years following his visions, Jung was caught up in psychic processes that involved a breakdown of categories such as inner and outer, and he went through a very real personal breakdown that simulated psychosis (auditory hallucinations, talking to invisible figures, extreme emotional states etc.) but, unlike madness, Jung's ego remained intact. He was able to reflect upon, as well as undergo the breakdown of categories.

His written record of this journey is now published as *The Red Book*. [3] Jung's understanding of what he went through is

---

[2]   Jung, C. G. (1963). *Memories, Dreams, Reflections*. New York: Random House. P. 175 ff.

[3]   Jung, C. G. (2009). *The Red Book*. (S. Shamdasani, Ed., S. Shamdasani, M. Kyburz, & J. Peck, Trans.) New York: W.W. and Norton & Company.

complex and beyond the scope of this book, but we can touch on two aspects that are relevant here. [4] On the one hand, after Jung emerged from his immersion in the "breakdown", he returned to the categories of inner and outer and took up the question of how one could have anything to do with the other. For example, his theory of synchronicity is a sustained attempt to find a theoretical connection between inner events, say a dream, and a "coincidental" event in the outer world. On the other hand Jung seemed to accept the breakdown of categories (e. g. spatial and temporal categories that form the structure of modern consciousness) and to change accordingly in his self-definition. He thus became *initiated* by the experiences themselves into a new reality. This initiation gave Jung the power to form new conceptions appropriate to this reality and thus perceive new aspects of the real world. These new conceptions gave rise to his unique notion of soul as absolute interiority—a conception subsequently fully developed by Wolfgang Giegerich. [5]

Jung's complex and contradictory responses to the "breakdown of categories", have given rise to conflicting theoretical and methodological paths within the Jungian community but may be sympathetically understood as the result of a pioneer's attempt to face the sheer terror of participating in a breakdown of the very categories that support modern consciousness itself. And, if consciousness itself is undergoing a transformation, then personal breakdowns and world convulsions are highly likely, as our history demonstrates so well. [6]

One of the significant category breakdowns that is relevant to my articulating the "genre" of writing that this book

---

[4] For a detailed analysis, see Giegerich, W. (2010). "Liber Novis, that is, The New Bible, A First Analysis of C. G. Jung's Red Book". *Spring 83*, 361-413.

[5] See, for example, Giegerich, W. (2012). *What is Soul?* New Orleans. Spring Journal Inc.

[6] For a detailed analysis of this process see Woodcock, J. C. (2013). *Overcoming Solidity: World Crisis and the New Nature.* Bloomington. iUniverse.

is concerned with is that of the pair of opposites: doing and reflection. Within our modern structure of consciousness we consider these a pair of opposites. We can do something in life or reflect on something in life but not both at the same time.

In the kind of writing I am suggesting it seems that both happen simultaneously or something else happens that subsumes both within itself. I call this "happening" *participation.*

Participation with the background process of category breakdown is reflection and doing, yet neither. Thus, participation can be sharply distinguished from automatic writing where the writer's consciousness plays no part. It is also different from having an experience and subsequently writing about that experience from memory. The writing that emerges from this participatory process therefore is a form (it's probably too early to call it a genre) that *embodies* such category break downs (inner-outer, past-present-future, action-reflection, etc.)

To this extent such writing will appear crazy, as writers of this emerging form are forced to express mind-bending notions that are faithful to the phenomenon yet incoherent when subjected to the requirements of our stable modern form of consciousness.

I recently saw an example of such "nonsense" when I was awake, late at night, unable to sleep. I was being besieged by these and other crazy thoughts. I turned on the TV and to my surprise saw a re-run of *Terminator* (1984). The heroine (Sarah) and her rescuer are being chased by the Terminator and are resting in a tunnel where she seeks to understand the logic of what is happening. The machines had sent a Terminator back through time to kill her so that she cannot give birth to the hero and then train him in warfare to save future humanity from the machines. The mere presence of this future machine forces this simple waitress to gain the very skills that the machines fear, and to become pregnant with the "saviour". Her rescuer had been arrested and a forensic psychologist listened to his story of travel from the future. He declared the prisoner completely delusional. The heroine, however, is willing to listen as he talks, not of futures, but *possible futures*. From their point of view, now in the Present, they are confronted with possible futures penetrating the Present (in the form of the Terminator who is only one *possible* future) and their actions matter, although they cannot predict the outcome (whether Sarah would be killed or not).

It seems from this and other like examples that the idea of possible futures intersecting with the Present and demanding action, without knowing the outcome, becomes important only when the usual categories that support present-day consciousness break down.

There are many such instances of art forms now that are "speaking" this way and seem to be engaging the contemporary artistic mind. One such book is the compelling example of *The Exegesis of Philip K. Dick*, which is a partial collection of the "mad" writings of science-fiction writer, Phillip K. Dick, (*Blade Runner, The Minority Report*). [7] This book gives us a glimpse of his eight years-long immersion into the background of consciousness as long-held categories break down.

In 1974, Dick had a revelation which ignited a superhuman feat of writing constantly over a long series of nights, running to eight thousand pages, a "sudden, discorporating slippage into vast and total knowledge that he would spend the rest of his life explicating, or exegeting." [8] The posthumous publication of some of these texts highlights Dick's long and arduous attempt to understand what exactly was happening to him, in a similar manner to C. G. Jung's efforts, as recorded

---

[7] Dick, P. K. (2011). *The Exegesis of Philip K. Dick*. (P. L. Jackson, Ed.) New York: Houghton Mifflin Harcourt.

[8] From the Introduction.

in his Red Book. I can choose any page at random to get a feel for sheer movement taking place, on-rushing fervour, a furore, gathering rapids, as punctuation breaks down, or ceases really to matter, as an onrushing life begins to prevail. It's like navigating a maelstrom at times, with little islands emerging only to be swept away again. The structure of that book is described as "a freewheeling voice that ranges through personal confession, esoteric scholarship, dream accounts, and fictional figures . . . one of the most improbable and mind-altering manuscripts ever brought to light." [9]

When I compared this description of Dick's writing with that of my own (see above), I knew that we had some common ground. For starters, I also underwent a prolonged "meltdown" in which the very categories that support our present-day consciousness dissolved. I was also forced to write my way out of it and then I learned the way out is *via* the way in. I had to participate more deeply in the material that was presenting itself to me, as Dick had to, as well.

A key methodological approach in producing this kind of "mad" writing is that the author takes seriously whatever phenomenon presents itself, *in its own terms*. The author must be able to remain "within" the phenomenon long enough so that it can teach her what it means in terms of its own logic, no matter how crazy it may sound when appraised from the categories of our current form of consciousness. The author is thus compelled to think self-presentational thoughts that defy rationality. I'll give one example here from Dick's book, *Valis*, which I also read with enormous enthusiasm, subsequently to writing this book.

---

[9]   From the Flyleaf.

Dick tells us of a dream he had in which he is living with his wife: [10]

> I have had dreams of another place myself, a lake up north and the cottages and small rural houses north and the cottages and small rural houses around its south shore. In my dream I arrive there from Southern California, where I live; this is a vacation spot, but it is very old-fashioned. All the houses are wooden, made of the brown shingles so popular in California before World War Two. The roads are dusty. The cars are older, too.

Following the dream, which Dick accepts completely in its own terms, he begins to compare its reality with his outer reality which does not include many of the elements in the dream. He then gets a memory of his father and realizes that in his dream he is living his father's life. From this achievement, Dick argues further that the individual contains the history not only of her personal life but of our entire race, back to its origins, back to the stars: "This is gene pool memory, the memory of the DNA."

This final thought has been discovered and articulated by others. In modern times, C. G. Jung has developed a unique view of history which is very close to Dick's, namely that we are psychologically the "outcome" of many historical transformations in consciousness, all of which may be reconstructed in our modern minds, with the correct methodology—history, as much as it is psychologically relevant to our lives, may be found "within". [11] The really significant point here that I want to make is that Dick did not gain this knowledge externally, as

---

[10] Dick, P. K. (2010-04-18). *Valis* (S.F. MASTERWORKS). Orion. Kindle Edition. P. 113 ff.

[11] For a detailed discussion of this unique view of history see Giegerich, W. (2008). Collected English Papers Volume III: *Soul Violence*. New Orleans. Spring Journal Inc.

a student of psychology might do so. He was *initiated* into it by the phenomenon—his dream, which he took to be as real as his waking life! His eyes were opened to another reality!

To take this line of argument a step further, we can ask what ultimately happens if, when the very categories that support our current form of consciousness break down, we stay immersed in the chaos that logically follows, as Dick does and as I did (in my case for about fifteen years or so). The process at first becomes mad and both *Exegesis* and *Valis* feel that way, from the perspective of our modern-day consciousness. But Dick emerges with an astounding conclusion—one that I am totally in agreement with, on the basis of my own mad immersion: Dick discovered that a reversal in a fundamental polarity takes place.

Let me explain.

For thousands of years we have slowly stabilized a form of consciousness that has a structure of order/disorder. Consciousness is order and, outside, beyond the boundary, is disorder, chaos, evil, etc. Consciousness at first had to be periodically consumed by disorder and then renewed. It could not, for many generations, be relied upon to last forever. The dark irrational powers were a constant threat to the order of daylight consciousness and had to be held at bay by ritual acts of warding off. They also periodically had to be given their day—a day ritualized, for example, by the ancient Saturnalia or the Celtic Day of the Dead.

Over time our daylight consciousness became stabilized enough for these rituals to lose their power and necessity. Today they have degenerated into Halloween, etc. They have no psychological value. So now, we live in a stable world of rationality which is occasionally threatened by events evaluated as irrational (emotions, visions, delusions, the psychoses, etc.), all of which are dealt with primarily by medications and thus "warded off" (literalized by psychotic patients being put in the "back wards"). The content of irrational outbursts (or more accurately, *in*bursts) are not listened to or trusted in any way by the "healing profession". [12]

With this context we can more easily gain access to Dick's discovery. He shows us that if we take madness seriously and in a sustained way; if we take it on its own terms, as it presents itself to us, then the fundamental polarity that has driven our Western culture for thousands of years, giving rise, finally to our modern structure of consciousness—the rational-irrational polarity—reverses itself!

Astounding!

Dick outlines this reversal in his cosmogony: [13]

> The single most striking realization that Fat had come to was his concept of the universe as irrational and governed by an irrational mind, the creator deity. If the universe were taken to be rational, not irrational, then something breaking into it might seem irrational, since it would not belong. But Fat, having reversed everything, saw the rational breaking into the irrational. The immortal plasmate had invaded our world and the plasmate was totally rational, whereas our world is not.

What this means for us is this: Where we feel most sane is where we are in fact now insane. Our modern consciousness has so far isolated itself from everything else (the private self) that it is now psychotic—yet, of course, it thinks of itself as totally sane. Furthermore those aspects of our psychological

---

[12] There have been notable exceptions in the past, and I refer to one such endeavour (disguised) here in my book.

[13] Dick, P. K. (2010-04-18). *Valis* (S.F. MASTERWORKS). Orion. Kindle Edition.) P. 112.

being, now *persona non grata*—dreams, visions, "accidents", etc.—are the harbours of the very sanity that can cure us of the insanity of psychological isolation.

This is also my conclusion, based on many years of immersion in "madness", and taking them every bit as seriously as Philip K. Dick does, until they restored me to sanity.

This kind of writing demands both reflection and doing, i.e., what I earlier called participation! The ability of the author to engage this way probably determines the extent to which he could legitimately be called mad. The doing is a needing to act without knowing the outcome in the sense that modern consciousness knows (subject-object knowing). If we know the outcome then obviously we are merely repeating the past in some way, since present-day consciousness *knows* only in terms of the past (memory). This "doing" can at first be frightening to those who feel the "demand" to act in this way. Yet one can get used to it and even become curious.

If we participate with possible futures as they penetrate the Present, does it matter *how* we act in relation to them? If it did not matter then we would be forced to acknowledge a deterministic universe or an "intelligent designer", but possible futures more speak of a dark urge that agitates, burrows, seeking to "get ahead" or to enter material reality by finding any available opening. Philosophically we could talk of this process as a union of teleology and contingency. Wounded individuals, like me, are such available openings and the dark urge simply enters. It is up to the individual to survive the onslaught as the "burrowing spirit" works its way into the world. And it is up to the individual to develop those soul capacities that will assist the actualization of possible futures in forms that support biological and cultural life, rather than destroy it. There are many casualties of this impersonal process and the record of such encounters constitutes culture in its many varied forms. [14]

The impersonal nature of the burrowing spirit was brought home to me by a dream I had many years ago. In this dream:

> I am on a winding road in the country. I see a young woman throwing a boomerang in a field and it comes my way. I pick it up and throw it. This attracts her and she comes my way and joins me. We go by some animals and see a calf split off from the herd, alone and bleating for its mother. It is near a snake. The cobra rears up and it is golden and climbs easily onto the calf's back. The calf can barely take the weight and can do no more than try not to collapse.

This dream frightened me.

The snake, as the burrowing spirit, when it enters the world, must rest on a foundation (serpent wrapped around the world, or egg, on a turtle's back, tree etc.). But these *chthonic* aspects, as psychological realities, are today the most undeveloped aspects of the consciousness that gives rise to our modern Western culture and, thus, the psychological foundation is weak. D. H. Lawrence is one modern writer who saw this issue but could offer only a literalized solution to it. He was not able to see it as a psychological problem involving the deepest levels of our modern consciousness.

It appears that our species depends on a certain development taking place quickly and this fact shows up as images of the young, weak, and immature. A huge transformation in consciousness is taking place, supported on a relatively weak base. Such a

---

[14] For a fuller discussion of this aspect of individual participation, see Woodcock, J. C. (2013). *Manifesting Possible Futures: towards a new genre of literature*. Bloomington. iUniverse.

structure generates a feeling, on the human level, of being too young, bearing too much responsibility, being abandoned or let down by parents, left to assume responsibilities that one is not prepared for. Picasso's *Minotauromachy* pictures this precarious situation: The monster approaches civilization and everyone flees except a young girl who stands to meet him, with a light in one hand and some flowers in the other.

All this appears in my dream, as it does in Dick's *Valis* where the protagonist, Horselover Fat, is paired with feminine figures who are dying, ill, frail, and in need of "rescuing", unable to cope. In my case, although the situation was dire, there was also the possibility of the calf making it and growing into a mighty bull which can thus easily support the serpent. I held onto that possibility for many years as I slowly learned to assume the burden of the cobra. [15] The impersonal nature of the burrowing spirit can easily be seen in the fact that the calf was not special in any way. It simply met the criteria needed for the burrowing spirit to "get in", i.e., alienation, isolation, neediness, and therefore, availability.

I am now reminded of a little book that Owen Barfield wrote, in which he encounters his version of the burrowing spirit in the form of an invisible visitor with whom Barfield enters discussions. At the very end of the book, Burgeon (Barfield's literary ego) asks the Meggid why he was chosen by the angel. The Meggid answers simply: [16]

> Have you supposed you are the only one? There are others,
> whom you will find, if you have not done so already . . .
> The two holocausts have touched you comparatively

---

[15] For a fuller account, see Woodcock, J. C. (2011). *The Imperative.* Bloomington. iUniverse.

[16] Barfield, O. (1965). *Unancestral Voice.* Middletown. Wesleyan University Press.

> lightly, the reigns of terror not at all . . . Many would have been reached before you [but for the holocausts]. The area of our choice at present is not so wide.

The following story, *UR-image*, thus belongs to the "genre" of writing that springs from, and expresses, the burrowing spirit as it makes its way into actuality through the psychological "wounds" of individual human beings. Where I had once been terrified in writing this way, I am now more curious, and thus, it seems, the demand has become gentler, less invasive, but still insistent.

The logical structure of the story is that of four possible futures intersecting and informing the Present, shaping it and, finally, *becoming* the actual future of four young adventurers, but in ways that none of them could have predicted.

Finally, before we enter the story, I must offer some evidence of congruence between the content of the story that will soon unfold for you, the reader, and the way it came into being. This is not a story *about* such breakdowns in fundamental categories, as endured by other people. It is a story that *emerged* from my own participation in a possible future, i.e., the burrowing spirit. So, its completion has become *my* actual future, although as I say, I could not predict or plan this outcome.

This is how it came about.

It began with a dream—a dream as a possible future!

In this dream three pioneers of depth psychology appear, each representing a different comprehension of the nature of image, a question that has a long and venerable history. I begin to wonder if I could write a book about them and their ideas. As I do so, the German word, "Ur", starts to repeat itself to me, running through my mind, as I sleep. I become enthusiastic about writing a story of these three men in relation to image, a simple story that brings out the difference in their understanding of image. I also am looking around for some electronic leads that will help some wires connect to my speaker system so that I can be heard better.

I woke up with "Ur" resounding in me. I started to look around for some "electronic leads". I went to a search engine and typed in "Ur" and found that the word means "original", "primitive" (meaning primary or basic). This awakened a memory and, according to the methodology of participation, I did not ignore but included it as the "next step". Years ago I had written an essay, out of another participatory moment with a possible future, in which I stumbled onto what I then called the form of forms which gives rise to all phenomenal forms. This discovery literally came out of my hands which moulded clay while my mind was in a breakdown and I was in a blind panic.

This memory startled me as it seemed I had been, in retrospect, talking about an Ur-image, as I named it in the moment of recall—an Ur-image, the original image that has to be non-phenomenal and yet which gives rise to all images.

I had the title of my book. Then, another surprise!

The same search turned up another result. A kindle book had been recently published. It was Stephen King's short story for Kindle, about Kindle, and it was called *Ur*. I quickly downloaded it and read it. It was a book dedicated to the notion of alternative universes and the possibility of their intersecting with our Present. I realized that the idea of alternative universes is a spatial conception having the same weird logic as the temporal conception of possible futures.

Another memory then came "out of left field". A famous author once said (I cannot remember who), "Write what you know."

And so, I began to write.

CONTENTS

1965: APPEARANCE

There is a world of forces which mould a form again and again in streaming repetition, while material substance becomes gradually assimilated into it. The . . . form slowly and gently appears, as though surrounded and permeated by invisible streams . . . the creation of form, purely through movement.

Theodore Schwenk

EDGAR LOVED TO SURF. HE was a board rider long before *Billabong* and a host of other companies managed to commodify and institutionalize this freedom into a sport with international contests and world-wide fashions. Oh, Ed was quite aware of the secondary social gains accruing from surfing that were, even then, in place. He knew that the large calloused knobs on his knees were in fact badges of his commitment and dedication and he wore them proudly. He also made sure that he did not shower immediately after a morning ride so that the salt would continue to bleach his hair just the right tones, publically marking him as a *bona fide* surfer. He was careful not to wear the white zinc oxide sun protection at any cost in order not to be mistaken as the enemy who arrogantly smeared it liberally across nose and cheeks, probably as a declaration of war. The battle lines between surfers and life guards were drawn and moved in perfect accord with the riptides and red flags that marked out the best areas for swimmers, banning surfers forever. Invariably the flags were erected each morning in precisely those areas where the waves displayed the best tubes, breaking perfectly on the waist-high sandbars, thus leaving choppy waters and sweeping tidal shifts to the board riders, often sweeping them a kilometre down the beach—out of the way, no doubt, of the sight of the enemy!

Ed hated the life guards because, as a surfer, he had to, in order to align himself with the best surfers at school and on the waves. Ed did not really hate anyone. His concerns were of another order altogether. He woke up each morning in eager anticipation, listening intently outside his window. He was attuned to the sound that the waves made and knew exactly what kind of wave he could expect. A soft sharp crack in the distance was the best sound. This meant that the wind was still blowing off-shore with an out-going tide creating tubes that broke crisply and perfectly on the long sandbank. No long or exhausting paddling. You just walk out, dive under the breaking line and there you are, floating freely in the ocean watching the swells approaching, lining up beautifully. It was exhilarating!

Ed's concerns of another order were not conscious. You could say that they appeared as the world appeared to him. Each day he got out of bed, grabbed his board before his parents woke up and headed down the empty street towards the large grassy park that faced the vast stretch of beach looming up behind the sand hills. He could sometimes see comrades already enjoying the rides further along the beach—much further along, way down the beach, too far to go. He thus entered the water alone and for the next hour or so before school would catch ride after ride, sometimes spectacularly so but always alone, with a persistent subliminal fear of what lay beneath the surface of the water, as measured by the frequency with which he would pull his feet out of the water and look about for the tell tale dorsal fin that would confirm his cautionary stance.

This, then, was Ed's world and it represented his deepest concerns—his desire for the thrill of the ride, and his terror of the depths.

Gary and Al attended the same school as Ed and were even in the same classroom, as they had been born in the same year.

Ed was always in the middle of the action, whatever it was and so it was he, on this particular day, who put the thumbtack on McMullan's chair just as his monumental bulk lurched and subsided into place, thus setting a chain of events in motion that were to change the lives of four friends forever.

When nothing happened, it was Gary who worked out that the tack must have been situated exactly so that each McMullian cheek settled gelatinously on either side of it, swallowing up the miniature spear completely. It could now make its dangerous point only to what the boys imagined was a dark, empty, and forbidding cave.

Al felt sorry for Michael. He could sense his loneliness and had tried many times to reach out to him. But, as things go at the typical Australian school, Michael McMullan only had eyes for the "leaders of the pack" and regularly sucked up to the Wayne Goldsteins and Oscar Turnbulls who led the way in academics and sports at Mermaid Beach High.

Gary felt no such pity. His joy was to figure things out and so he set about drawing a diagram of the physics of the situation, showing it to Ed who chortled out loud, adding a few foul details before giving it to the uncomprehending McMullan, just before the teacher snatched it up, yelling to the boys, "I told you to get on with your work. Now do it!"

Such imperatives were completely lost on the boys who were mesmerised by the pendant their young, voluptuous teacher wore around her neck. It lay gently nestled between two mounds of an entirely different kind which excited Ed's imagination in quite another direction than those of McMullan. It was he that noticed the peculiar configuration of the two spherical pearls that hung so enticingly in what was surely a perfumed valley of delights. "I bet they belonged to her ex-husband," he whispered to Al who felt faintly embarrassed by such explicit references expressed in not so *sotto voce*.

"What was that?" "Why don't you share your thoughts with us all Allen?" "It wasn't me Miss," complained the now furious victim of circumstances. "Very well, we'll discuss this after school. You are going to stay behind with me. And who drew this disgusting picture? Was that you, too?"

"Ask her about the balls," Ed snickered across the aisle with all the skill of a ventriloquist so that, this time, it was Gary who earned the privilege of explaining himself after school with the delectable Miss Monkhouse. "But Miss, that wasn't me. You know how sound travels in moist air. It couldn't have been me that you heard from that particular angle where you are sitting."

His classmates groaned. They were used to this. "Einstein" was at work again. Gary had earned this derisively bestowed honour one day when, after a heated discussion with his physics teacher, he had shouted at no one in particular, "Well, they called Einstein wrong too!" He could not back this assertion with any evidence but it felt satisfying even if it doomed him to a perpetual feeling of being patronized by others—as he was now being patronized by the entire class for his well-worked out explanation of the obvious mistake of the teacher in apportioning blame to him.

He was also called Gazza, or better yet, Azzag, according to the time-honoured classroom ritual of saying a name backwards in order to further humiliate anyone who got in the line of fire. Everybody's favourite target in this regard was the relatively harmless Pat Morris who transformed, upon reversal, like Clark Kent into Superman, into the redoubtable *Sirromtap*!

"I'll let you know how the waves are breaking," came the relentless commentary, materializing it seemed, out of thin air.

"OK, I have had enough! You can stay back too, young Edgar Peacock," snapped Miss Monkhouse who finally got her bat-like sonar to hone in on the real culprit. The boys, however, were instantly distracted by the deliciously violent manner in which her jewellery suddenly heaved up and down like two marker buoys on the only waves that Ed was going to experience that day. O yes, indeed! Man overboard!

"Miss! Miss! Isn't there another way? They are coming to my birthday party today."

A hush settled over the room. Miss Monkhouse, stalling momentarily like a dive bomber at the top of its loop, was gaping slightly at this unexpected, and most unwelcome, questioning of her iron will. But the boys were turned as one towards the calm, assured, and not the least offensive, voice of one Miss Poesy Pond, who was called Po' by all. It wasn't so much the blatant lie that bestirred the boys. It was the dulcet sound of her voice! Ed heard faint echoes of waves whispering against a sandy shore with the incoming tide, promising pleasures of long graceful rides; Gazza was certain that, one day, he would finally understand how the mere sound of her voice, no matter *what* she said, could spontaneously evoke images in his mind that he had not thought up himself. Right now, he could picture a *way*, which became a road. This image associated to the word "method"—yes, *hodus*, a journey! Of course! Po' is going to show me a method . . .

Al simply melted. He too, was besieged by images whenever Po' spoke. The most enduring image that he nurtured was one of rescue. He frequently imagined that the school was burning down and that Po' was on the roof of the last standing building, in distress and calling for help. He in turn was always standing below, shouting, "Jump! Jump! I will catch you. You can trust me! It's alright Po', I will catch you! Jump!"

"What do you mean, 'chump', you rude boy?" Time suddenly broke back in with Miss Monkhouse's jaw snapping shut and Po's quick infectious giggle filling the room with the scent of jasmine, as it seemed to the now disoriented and blinking

Allen Benjamin. He was shaken free of his drugged reveries by the inevitable cat calls. He was now doomed to be cursed by *Nimajneb Nella*.

The outcome was clear and obvious to all. Party or no, there were now four, all for one and one for all, as Al liked to imagine at times, who were to enjoy the imposing company of one Miss Monkhouse for the next hour after the final bell rang that day.

This chain of events, or was it cluster, maybe conglomerate, led Gary, much later on, to wonder if there were more to it than sheer accident of randomness at work. Be that as it may, this day, pretty much like any other day in the lives of school boys and girls at Mermaid Beach High, became a *kairos* for the intrepid Three Musketeers, as Al liked to imagine himself and his friends. More exactly, the *kairos* opened up on the way home, as they strolled down the dusty road, discussing what feasible story would satisfy the predictable parental worries and accusations about school behaviour or out-of-school shenanigans.

"I know," volunteered Gazza, "we can say that we were working on a physics project at school. How about something to do with the Coriolis effect? But we have all got to make sure we tell the same story. Our parents will be impressed!"

"Shit, it's too late to catch the evening tide," moaned Ed, "so we might as well take our time, enjoy the sunset. Look the wind is picking up! That will flatten the waves for sure. Listen, Gazza! I know all about Coriolanus. We studied it at school. It's all about revenge. That's where the phrase, 'Revenge is a dish best served cold' came from. That's what we should be talking about. How to get revenge on Monkeyhouse! We could lift her VW bug onto the concrete ledge . . ."

"You idiot! I said, 'Coriolis', not 'Coriolanus'! And besides, it wasn't Coriolanus who said that, it was Titus Andronicus who *did* that by serving a pie of human meat. I am not talking about

8

revenge. I am talking about the earth's rotation and its effect on the weather patterns."

"Aaah, my poor Athos," thought Allen to himself. He randomly assigned Musketeer names to his friends, most often giving himself the distinction of being D'Artagnon, the fourth and most handsome. This assignment of course locked in Po's identity as either Milady de Winter or Constance, both of whom suffered a fateful tragedy. He glanced over to her, as she wheeled her bicycle alongside the boys.

"Milady, whence such dark hair? Art thou the Black Swan too? Art thou Constant in love?" A stubbed toe broke his reverie just in time to hear Aramis, or is it Porthos today, speak:

". . . no, seriously, if we can agree on this we will convince our parents. They haven't got a clue what the Coriolis Effect is. They'll believe us. Trust me!"

"Dear Gazza, none of us, save you, know. How can we go . . . ?"

"Dearest Constance," Al's reverie resumed, "You cannot help yourself can you? Rhymes drip from your lips. And such lips! Libidinous sap of the muses, I must save you. I must . . ."

"Why are you limping, Al? And are you listening to me? I have a plan for us all. Look! Let's get this together. Po', don't worry about it. You can make half of it up. Just know that the Coriolis Effect is the earth's rotation which determines the direction that weather patterns take as they move over the surface of oceans. Cyclones rotate anti-clockwise in the Northern hemisphere as a result. Here they rotate clockwise. Oh and by the way forget the shit about water going down drains any particular way. That's all bullshit!"

"Al, *you're* bullshit. That's what we all know," complained Ed. "I'm missing some good rides now and you want me to think about *this* shit."

"It's your fucking fault, *Ragde*, you moron. Playing Chinese whispers in class got us all into trouble. And I'm trying to think a way out for us all."

"No, no, it's so easy." This from Po'. "All we need agree is that our parents must see that we were planning a party." Al almost swooned at this flood of alliteration. He couldn't speak. So he just nodded. Anything you say, Po' . . .

At this moment, the very moment that was to become the fateful *kairos* in the lives of these four intrepid chums, Ed noticed an appearance in the road, right in front of them, just as the sun was setting in the red dust of the Australian horizon.

"Look! Look," he exclaimed. "It's a dust devil. Just beginning!"

About ten meters ahead, a small swirl of dust was forming in the middle of the road and began to wander towards them, gathering strength from the shifting winds and temperature gradients as day gave way to evening. Ed raced ahead yelling "Come on. I've always wanted to do this." Po's dark eyes lit up a faint red as they caught the last rays of sun. She watched Ed approvingly. She loved taking a risk and loved even more egging boys on to take the risk for her because then she could take maximum advantage of both worlds at once—the world of engagement and the world of aesthetic appreciation. Al watched enviously. Why couldn't she look at me that way? Smouldering eyes of love gazing at the knight racing off to adventure for her sake, wearing her favour on his sleeve . . .

Gazza shouted out to all: "The velocity of the wind increases inversely to the radial distance from the centre so that you'll really feel it the more you enter it. They say there is a still point at the very centre which must mean there is a discontinuity somewhere . . ." Gary knew something about this. He had once volunteered to save some beach houses on the coast when a cyclone was bearing down on the area. Winds were screaming overhead as he and others frantically packed sandbags and shoved them under exposed foundations while the abnormally high tides swept away the landfill. Then suddenly, it all had fallen eerily silent. It was unnerving. Gary learned later that they were momentarily in the eye of the storm. Then, the winds picked up again only now they were shrieking in the opposite direction. It went on for hours and Gary had never forgotten it. He was proud that he now knew what the inside of a cyclone was like. He could explain it to others and was now doing so to Ed, or maybe more to Po', since Ed was some distance away and probably could not hear him. He was facing the dust devil directly now, his attention riveted, and his friends had to catch up as best they could.

The small wind whipped at Ed's clothes and a faint orange glow was imparted to his tousled hair, giving it an appearance of being on fire. Po' was simply delighted as she ran towards him shouting, "Go on. You know you want to. You do, you know. Go, Go!"

Both she and Gazza ran apace while Al trotted behind wrestling with the bigger demon of mounting jealousy, verging on rage, as his beloved Constance betrayed his love with every excited step towards who could now only be the evil Cardinal Richelieu.

"Constance! I doubt it," as Milady de Winter settled into his soul, finally freezing all feeling.

Ed stood on the edge of the dust devil, gazing into the very centre where he could see a strange silent light, like a beacon on the ocean during a dark and stormy night. It was blue-violet to the point of being black. "I must remember that line," he thought wryly. "Al will like that. It's his corny style." He could faintly hear Po's entreaties and Gazza's waving arms. What was she saying? No, No?—No way! Nobody is going to stop me having this experience. I've waited a long time for this. What the hell is Gazza going on about? Oh, screw him!" Just as the sun finally gave up the ghost and was lost behind the gathering clouds, Ed took the fateful step and, along with the last tendrils of daylight clinging to the swollen edges of the *Cumulus Nimbus*, he was extinguished.

"Impossible," said Gazza as he and the others arrived breathlessly to the point where they last saw their errant friend. The dust devil was moving off and beginning to lose strength although the strange light emanating from its centre persisted. "Couldn't he see? What is wrong with that idiot? Why couldn't he hear me? Don't you guys get it? There is something wrong. The dust devil is turning the wrong way. It's going anti-clockwise!" And that light in the centre . . . It can't be reflected light. It must be self-originating light. But that is impossible! And where is he? He can't be gone. He must be here somewhere."

Struggling with the strange mix of suddenly revived feeling, Al blurted out insincerely, "Let's look for him, then. You go over there and Po' and I will search back here."

Po' dismissed this paltry attempt to woo her, cutting Al to the quick. She was pointing wide-eyed to the dust devil. "Don't you both see? His moment arrived and he stepped into it. It was his time."

"He must have stepped *through* it," said Gary, trying to find some reason not to be afraid.

"No, No!' he stepped *into* it and the light glowed more brightly and Ed seemed to contract into its intensity. He is gone and we must follow him."

"There must be a better explanation than that. Look I'll go into it and show you." Gary took a deep breath to avoid breathing the whirling dust and leaped into the centre. With the same brief display of intense light, he disappeared.

For one mad self-serving moment Al realized that he was at last alone with Po' but before he could say anything he might regret later, she grabbed his hand and pulled him violently towards the dust devil. By now the sky was dark and the ambient temperature was settling into its night-time shift. The dust devil was losing power and had wandered off the road into the bush. "Come on!" Po' shrieked. "It's too late. It's going."

Just holding her hot urgent hand gave Al the courage he needed even if it was backed by completely mistaken assumptions about possible futures with Po'. Together they leaped. The light at the centre of the dust devil gave one last burst of energy and then the whole structure collapsed with barely a sigh.

Night finally closed in.

A bicycle and three school packs were left scattered along the road. Cicadas soon resumed their deafening washer board music. Frogs accepted this cue for love and began their own version of a mating song which lasted somehow throughout the long night. Around midnight, a solitary dingo came to the side of the road, waited, then ambled over to the fallen school packs. He sniffed, waited, looked up, heard a small animal shuffle in the darkness off to one side, and moved on in the direction of a likely meal, melting silently into the Australian bush.

1995: EDGAR

Now, so entire is my faith in the power of words, that, at times, I have believed it possible to embody even the evanescence of fancies such as I have attempted to describe.

Edgar Allen Poe

EDGAR WAS A MASTER OF the hypnogogic state. This did not mean that he could control it, or that he could manipulate his comings and goings to and from that state. He did, however, cultivate the state and he knew what to do when he sensed its approach.

It always began softly, a whisper. This night, Edgar was lying on his back in bed, awake yet, once again, curiously powerless to move. This was to be expected and, although he was not alarmed, he was at once anxious and filled with anticipation.

The presence grew more strongly as vibrations, an echoing sound with a definite beat, even wasps or bees. Louder and louder, more insistent! Images of wings, insects, wasps, or simply waves came to consciousness and quickly passed. Now Edgar's body began to shake violently. His spine had become a coil and was winding tighter and tighter. A wave broke over him on him and the coil released, sending a deep shudder through him. A crescendo of beating wings crashed over him and then, silence. Edgar's senses were fully awake and he could see about him in the room. He also knew that his eyes were closed and that he was asleep. These contradictory facts guaranteed his successful entry into the hypnogogic state.

Over long years of practice, Edgar had learned to lower his fear of paralysis which had caused him to exert his will in order to wrench himself awake, often resulting in a tumble to the floor. He slowly had gained confidence that his body would continue its automatic functions, such as breathing, just as it does when we sleep normally. He could thus stay alert and wait, as he did this particular night.

The hypnogogic state had the peculiar quality of presenting the familiar world to Edgar in his paralysed *in-between* state of sleep. His could "see" his bed, furniture, and clothes lying loosely over a chair, for example but there were also significant differences such as the ceiling light which was now simply a naked bulb hanging down with remnants of Christmas ribbons still wrapped around it, quite unlike that of the waking state. Edgar had discussed these topological features, and more, with his good friend Gary, and they had concluded that the hypnogogic state, although undoubtedly a state of mind, was also insisting on a very close relationship between that state of mind and the form "outer" reality took, quite unlike the relationship that prevails in normal waking life today. The hypnogogic state could be described as a reality that lay *within* ordinary reality and which could demonstrate, through initiatory experience, a living connection between mind and world such that, as one changed, then the other had also. Gary had been very helpful in this regard, with his inquiring and precise mind, along with an enduring passion for truth and knowledge.

As Edgar reviewed his past discussions with Gary, he laid in bed quietly breathing and feeling what could only be described as a tension in the very air surrounding him. Something was "here"! He felt a presence within his very skin. Something was alive and co-extensive with his body. With a shock he realized there was a woman inside him, skin to skin, sharing his sensory-motor system. She began feel more and more distinct, separating herself from him although remaining joined to him. She began to kiss him, from the inside, making love to him. Edgar became aroused but also scared too. It was uncanny to have someone in his skin, sharing his body. He began turning in order to see her. He wanted to see her face to face but she resisted him. It wasn't a moral resistance but more like a magnetic field type of resistance. It was also like one body moving to two separate wills. Edgar managed to turn around and saw a young woman, now toe to toe, belly to belly, heart to heart with him, yet still sharing the one body. He gazed deeply into her eyes and saw the universe of stars. Thoughts of the Knights Templar raced through his mind. She then came out of his skin and stayed a little behind him, holding him down. He could physically feel her arms and body. He willed his way around again to face her and their mouths met. Hers was, as they say, like honey. A stray thought crossed his mind that he would have to save that trope for Allen who was enamoured of such poetic devices. As their mouths met, she resisted at first but her moistures were flowing. Edgar touched her and they began to make love. He could feel them both, yet as himself, as they moved together. She was distinguishable from him and yet she came out of him in some sense. Finally, Edgar felt the presence retreat and he fell into a light refreshing sleep until the following early morning.

Edgar was a wanderer. He lived by following the next wave of enthusiasm that struck him without really knowing where he would be taken. He just enjoyed the ride. He had little money and hated working for others so he was forced, to some degree, to live off his friends' largesse. His closest friends were Allen and Po' Benjamin. They had some rooms to spare since their twins had grown up and "flown the coop" as Al often quipped by way of one of his tiresome clichés. Edgar often stayed in the basement room where he could meditate and prepare for his nocturnal adventures with the hypnogogic state.

On this particular morning their mutual friend Gary arrived for breakfast, too. He had developed some ideas based on Ed's previous experiences with the hypnogogic state and was eager to share them before delivering a lecture to the Literary Society of Sydney. He was interested in outlining a new form of reality, or maybe a new art form. He believed that Ed's experiences, along with Allen and Po's subtle explorations of the psyche were demonstrating the seeds of an artistic possibility that could represent a transformation in reality taking place today. This literary form involves the author's entering a state of mind not unlike Ed's hypnogogic state. The author then receives or welcomes whatever "psychic visitor" presents itself to him, with no regard for ontological concerns such as "memory", "dream", "inner" or "outer", and with no regard for interpretation. This is where Allen and Po's work became an important contribution for Gary. Po' had an inexplicable gift for perceiving subtle forms in such a way that they would, at times, manifest, i.e. become visible to the one who was in this hypnogogic state. Allen, in turn enjoyed a profound trust in following the smallest invisible lead that presented itself to him, inwardly or outwardly, he didn't care, without knowing where it would take him. Gary often thought of Allen as a dog in this regard.

He was reviewing his thoughts in this way when Po' greeted him at the door and, once again, Gazza (no one could remember how *that* started) felt some momentary vertigo as he gazed into the deep blue-violet pools that were Po's eyes.

Po' could be looking at you in a perfectly ordinary manner and then, without warning, she could take you in, not in the sense of conning you, but in the sense of reading your very essence, way past what your ego would expect. She would keep what she saw to herself but you were left with an uncomfortable but faintly erotic feeling that you had been, for a moment, quite naked before her. She *could* con you with that knowing and sometimes did but it was always playful, unpremeditated and always left you, once again, with a feeling that she had been simply making love to you. Her speech was erotic. When she spoke, her words penetrated with generative intent, and the room became pregnant with meaning. Some of Gary's best ideas were born from such moments. He did not quite know how that could be but was always eager for the next tryst knowing that, for some reason, Allen never got jealous. Gary could not work that one out, either, but he swore that he would, one day.

Po' delivered Gary into Al's care in the kitchen while she went down to the basement to get Edgar. He should be awake now, she thought. She found him at the small rosewood desk, furiously writing.

"I mustn't forget this one," he said, barely lifting his head in acknowledgement of her unobtrusive knock-and-then-enter system of hospitality. It had taken both him and Gary a while to get used to her style. At first, when Po' had arrived into a room this way, bedroom, bathroom, whatever it was, she had often been greeted with a mad scramble to recover what was clearly forever-lost dignity, much to her amusement. Then, over time, both men came to realize that those dark blue-violet eyes were not judging anything at all. They were simply seeing and *what* they were seeing had very little to do with moral judgment. In time, Ed and Gary simply got used to being seen this deeply, this *imaginatively*, and they relaxed, perhaps more so than they thought possible in the presence of another human being, and a beautiful female human being at that.

Po' quietly drifted over to Edgar's chair and, again without asking permission, looked over his shoulder at the page of writing.

"We'll have something to talk about over breakfast, I see," she whispered.

Ed had woken up earlier and rushed to the desk to record his hypnogogic experience. So he was stark naked. More than this though, due to the particular nature of this experience, he exuded a heavy, musky male scent, like a cat on the prowl and Po' felt her own body stirring in resonant response. Where Edgar had gained a mastery of the hypnogogic state, however, Po' was mistress of her erotic life so she felt no need to act in any particular way but chose to breathe it all in, while Edgar continued to write. She no longer focussed on the fast moving pen. Instead she became dreamy. Her eyes lost their focus in this world and dilated. She was *seeing*. Her heightened but contained erotic energies became the bow from which she was released into visionary space.

She saw the vortex, briefly, and it was very black. And it was approaching.

Startled, she gasped and returned to the room where Ed suddenly got up and excused himself. She laughed gaily when she saw the problem. Where he had been writing, the words suddenly skewed off the page. In fact, while she had been momentarily transported by their interpenetrating energies, her hair had been trailing into Ed's ear, and, given his state of dress, along with his nocturnal adventure, Ed realized that he was getting distracted from writing in a most obvious and disturbing way.

While he was regaining some small degree of composure, Po' began to reflect on what she had just seen. We should discuss this at breakfast as well, she thought. Edgar returned in t-shirt, jeans and his old Birkenstocks, along with a faint blush. Without a word, they moved back upstairs to the kitchen where Allen and Gary had prepared coffee, pancakes and fried eggs.

Gary opened up the discussion, as soon as the gustatory tempo eased up. He poured himself another coffee, offered it around and, after hearing the satisfied demurrals, began.

"Look, I've given a great deal of thought to this. I for one accept the reality of Ed's experiences with the hypnogogic state. It's clear he is not just making this up. There is an objective process going on that he participates with and then writes down afterwards from memory. He also calls it the in-between-state and this feels right to me, too, although the wording of that is clumsy. It's not really "in between" two other states but is in itself a state, or reality. I just don't know what to make of it."

"Artists are familiar with this realm of reality" said Al, "and 'use it', if that's the right way to put it, to create their works of art. In this way we are able to get glimpse of what they know to be true. We can ask, 'where did such vision come from? And what is it speaking about? What does it want?' Artists often do not feel compelled to ask these questions or even resist it. They simply *express* it. Others, like Ed here seem simply to seek the experience of it."

"Well, yeh. Who wouldn't?" exclaimed Ed. And he then went on to recount his experience of the previous night to his spell-bound audience. By the time he was finished their coffee was cold and so Al got up to brew some fresh beans, while Ed regrouped a little, feeling somewhat exposed by the explicit nature of his nocturnal adventure. While he had been telling his story, Po' leaned back slightly and her eyes had acquired the far-away look that Al loved so dearly, and, if truth be told, feared a little too. You never knew what she would come back with.

Finally, she spoke, addressing Gary. "Gazza, Al and I have been doing some research on this matter as well. I think you are quite correct in your assessment that Ed, and others like him, are dealing with a *reality*. Ed's careful descriptions of his own experiences are also enormously helpful in getting us closer to the phenomenology of this reality. For example we can see that this reality is not concerned about an either-or logic, the logic that governs our current waking reality. So we have to use strange constructions like, "in-between-state", which you, Gazza, must find hardly satisfying. But *within* that reality, as Ed shows quite convincingly, things are simply 'just so' and Ed accepts them that way, participating fully and engaging with what is given him in the moment, fully and without skepticism. It's only when we come out of such states back into ordinary waking reality that the questions start to pile up. We try to comprehend that reality in the terms given us in *this* reality."

"It's mind-bending", interjected Gary, as he poured his third cup of coffee.

"Al and I are doing something a little different, though," she went on, "we are concerned with a kind of human participation that can be adequate to this new reality's *intention*!" Discerning Gary's immediate protest, as registered by the coffee spill onto the table, along with muttered apologies, she quickly went on. "I am not talking about a conscious process in which an 'entity' or some such (how she hated that word, so bandied about today) that has designs for us or for earth. No master plan! It's more like a dark urge that presses forward into the contingent world of matter and we human beings are indispensible to this process. Our participation with this dark urge determines the final form it takes in material reality. We only *know* when the producing has become the produced and we can thus reflect on it, just as Gazza does so well."

Al interrupted at this point. He was excited now. Po's words always had this effect on him. "Po' and I have no name as yet for this human participation but we are calling it a *new* kind for a couple of crucial reasons that arise from the kind of experiences that Ed explores so well. Now, art has always been the method by which the 'invisible' enters the material world, i.e. gains form. But here's what seems to be different today with experiences like Ed's. This dark urge that Po' refers to does indeed manifest in matter but this "matter" seems to be quite different to ordinary matter. And . . ."

"My god," interjected Edgar, "you have just given me an insight into a whole series of experiences I had in the hypnogogic state over many years, where I could actually move through walls, ceilings, floors. Their hardness was not impenetrable to me. They were clearly material but quite different to ordinary matter."

"It's this domain of reality that seems to be the "place" where the invisible can interpenetrate with the human being and thus gain form *in* the human being. It's as if the human being, *us*, has become the art form. Art form implies method and so Po' and I are developing a method of opening ourselves up to this process . . ."

"So that the invisible may incarnate in the "matter" of the human being, thus gaining access to the world through our sensory-motor system," interrupted Po'.

Both Edgar and Gary were leaning forward, tense with anticipation.

"This method that Al and I are trying to develop requires a new kind of mind, really. The best way I can get to it is by example. When Ed encountered his, what shall we say, *beloved*, last night, he remained true to his experience throughout and reported it faithfully to us this morning. Now what he does not know is that while he was writing his experiences down, there was a heightened energy in the room (Po's decided to omit certain details here for the sake of reducing unwanted, probably ribald, comments from the gallery), and I *saw something*."

Everyone knew what Po' meant when she *saw* something. She was in a visionary state.

"I saw a black tornado heading this way."

All eyes were on her now with rapt attention.

"Before we go into the kind of questions that Gazza might ask (no offence Gazza), I will tell you how I dealt with it in terms of the method that Al and I are developing. I saw that vision as belonging with Ed's experience last night, as does the energy that built up in the room—connected as with an invisible thread. Without knowing *what*, I accepted the connection and opened up to the whole thing working on me, *in* me, as it is still doing. The point is, for the method, not to go on with my life as if what had happened was an interesting story of no consequence to my actual concrete life, or that of others, but to start changing, according to the resonant effect induced in me from these threaded invisible happenings."

"In fact," said Al, I am writing a book that goes into this methodology in detail. I am trying to describe how a human life would look if one followed that method. I even have a trial name for it, along the lines that you would be familiar, Ed, the *flâneur*!"

"What's that?" said Ed.

Gazza spoke next. His knowledge of words and their etymology was considerable.

"Well, obviously it's French and it has a common meaning of loafing about, or slowing down enough to notice things that others speed by."

"Yes," said Al, "and I am bringing in a quality of noticing apparently disparate things that appear to the flâneur over a period of time, held together, as Po' says by an invisible thread. Over time, this thread will manifest into actuality, revealing what our Time really is all about. In fact if you take this method to the limit, there probably is a literary form that consists of all the hints that the flâneur has gathered, placed together without commentary, so that the hidden thread itself can emerge. At least that is what I am working on and I am doing it with quotations."

"What do you mean?" asked Gary, rapidly making connections between what Al was saying and his own investigations into a new literary form.

"I have always been fascinated by quotes and have gathered them over the years, probably as a flâneur might do. I have in mind one day to simply publish a book of these quotations. No commentary, just the quotes themselves, and see what emerges from that!"

"Not hoping to make much money from using other people's words, are you?" Ed's rhetorical question hung in the air mischievously.

"Well, only time will tell on that score, and speaking of time," Po' gracefully segued, "we have been talking non-stop for three hours. Its lunch time and I need to do some other things right now."

Everyone felt relieved at this shift in direction. Ed was exhausted from his inner journeys, Gazza was scribbling some notes on a napkin, and Al was eager to get alone with Po'. They had more to discuss, arising from this very fruitful discussion, and the nature of their discussion would probably, if history were any guide, take some equally fruitful turns that required privacy.

So Ed was sent off to his room to sleep some more and Gary left to go on some mission that most likely involved diving into his extensive library at home.

*   *   *

Allen and Po' lingered in bed together. It was now around 4 pm and the warm yellows of this Autumnal day were fading to grey. Now that the passions of a deep love were quenched, they simply laid there, breathing softly, draped casually at odd angles over each other's body with the familiarity of a long-time companionship. Po' stared at the ceiling while Al rested his head on her heart, relaxing into the steady drum beat until all thought vanished and there *was* only the beat: lub dub, lub dub, lub dub . . .

"Honey, your head is a bit heavy, would you mind . . . ?"

All things pass, he thought, obligingly shifting his weight.

"What are you thinking about, my darling?" he asked, now that the spell was broken.

"Well, I am thinking a bit about the black vortex approaching, coupled with Ed's experience last night," she replied softly.

"I love the verb you use, 'couple.'"

"Yes, as you and I know, eros is critical to our methodology for participation with possible futures."

"You were 'coupling' with Ed this morning down in the basement when you had this vision, weren't you?" inquired Al, although he knew the answer as well as she knew the sense in which such a startling claim was made.

"Yes, while he was writing, the erotic energy was strong so we know that the black vortex, the explicit images of coupling that Ed participated in, and production of the *language* of the experience, *as given by the experience*, belong together somehow."

"I was fascinated by Ed's description. Somehow he has learned how to unlearn thinking based on the past. He almost never imports theory into his descriptions of the hypnogogic state but listens to what presents itself in those very terms so that the description *becomes* the theory. He was forced to describe a movement of his mind in such imagistic terms probably because we don't yet have the language form . . ."

"A unity of difference clearly took place," Po' interrupted, "a unity in which the differences must be maintained in consciousness. But there is no eros in such language. It is an abstract dialectical formulation and the effect of such language is to take us up and out, away from the phenomenon that insists on real embodiment!" Po' was passionate now. "Some *invisible* 'wants' to embody in our sensory nervous system and Ed's experiences are precisely those that show the way. It seems to be in the form of a vortex right now."

"The vortex must be the approach of new language forms then," said Al, who was, by now, also alert and focussed.

"It would seem so," replied Po', who was becoming dreamy again. Just before she fell into another slumber, she softly added, so that Al had to strain to hear her, "the vortex is black."

1991: GARY

Living in the world of the Cartesian paradigm I know that matter is on the outside and spirit is in the inside and that they have an abyss between them. These realities are axiomatic, testable, and absolute.

that is until they break down.
until I break down
until the world breaks up
when what is so solid crumbles and dissolves
when what is so ethereal gains flesh and sinew

John Woodcock

THEY HAD HAD A FIGHT early in the morning. Gary was already being overwhelmed by ideas, thoughts, and images, spontaneously bursting into his conscious mind—had been for years. They arrived with such fury that his head was in a permanent inflammatory reaction. He struggled to cope with the deluge by studying as hard as could. He carried notebooks around with him because the visitations happened at any time of the day. He wrote down what came and then "went to the books" to find amplificatory ideas, some way to help him grasp what was happening. He was out of bed most nights, down in the basement, his head bursting with heat, sitting in a chair with the lights off. It was cooler down there and that was all he could think of doing.

When he stumbled upstairs this morning, barely greeting his wife and son, Po' simply reminded him to pick up some things at the store. He suddenly felt furious about the imposition, stormed out, and caught the bus into town where his office was located. And so, with this unpropitious beginning to the day, it all began to unravel.

Gary was a therapist and saw a few people in the central business district. He did belong to a professional organization and thus had a network of colleagues with whom he could speak but he could not bear to do so, most of the time. In between clients, he wrote. With each new flood of inner activity, he was sure he had the material for the next book, or at least the next essay to share with his colleagues and the wider world. The trouble was that no sooner had he fixed the flow into a set of relatively stable ideas, it would all be swept away again in a flood, leaving him stranded or drowning. He spent weeks, for example, reading one of C. G. Jung's most difficult books, *Aion*, with the driven idea that he could write a key to the book much in the same way that Joseph Campbell had written a brilliant key to Joyce's *Finnegan's Wake*, unpacking the various symbolic layers to give the reader more access to the book's wisdom. Gary tackled the task with fervour, writing down key obscure passages in *Aion*, and, next to them, literally sketching a small key with a number pointing to a page in a growing Glossary that he began to fill out with explanations and symbolic amplifications drawn from Jung's *Collected Works*.

To his horror, one day it stopped—the whole project just dried up. He could do nothing. The horror lay in the felt danger of being swallowed up by his inner life which was bursting at the seams. How can I keep on top of this, he thought agitatedly? And so it went on, like this. Renewed efforts to keep swimming on the oceanic upheavals were followed by more failures in output, enormous anxiety, and redoubling of intellectual effort. It was all Gary could do, and he was getting exhausted.

On this particular day, Gary climbed aboard the bus to go home. It was the middle of winter and snow was falling lightly. The bus driver cautiously negotiated the hilly incline. Fir trees lined the road, occasionally releasing their load of snow which then cascaded down in a shower of rainbow sparkles caught by the setting sun.

The bus came to a set of lights near a shopping centre, and slowed down further. An accident had occurred. Skid marks displayed the course of events quite clearly. A brown Mazda utility truck was wrapped around a tree and two bodies were laid out on the frozen ground, with blankets and coats that pedestrians had rushed to provide. Further away, another car, the one that had run the red light, was parked askew on the pavement with the driver holding his head in his hands, collapsed over the wheel.

It seemed to Gary that they were all going in silent slow motion. As the bus glided by, he looked for a long moment at the utility truck.

"Wait a minute, that's my truck," he snapped to the bus driver. "And that's my wife and son!"

"Do you want me to stop?" the bus driver wavered.

"Yes, yes, stop!" It was one of those insane moments in which different parts of the brain engage quite independently of each other. Gary simultaneously lunged for the door and scrabbled in his wallet to pay the ticket. He was waved away by the driver and leaped out of the bus to where Po', his wife and little Al, his only son, were resting on the snow-covered sidewalk.

Except they were not resting, they were dead.

Earlier that month, Gary had placed a large pine tree log in the back of the ute in order to weigh down the back end for the slippery conditions of winter. But it was not enough. When Po' tried to avoid the other car, she had slammed on the brakes and went into a spiral, turning three times before crunching into the tree, folding neatly around it.

*   *   *

It was now a year later. Gary still lived in the same house, alone. He didn't much care if the insert stove was working or not. If he happened to think of firing it up with some logs, he did so, but as often he would just put on an extra jumper and leave it at that. He continued seeing a few people professionally but otherwise remained at home, where he lived predominately at his desk, with a brown blanket for warmth. He had simply cut a hole out of the centre of this old blanket, making a makeshift poncho after the style of Clint Eastwood, "the man with no name". Just right, Gary had thought, as he roughly formed a circle, folded the blanket along the diameter before chewing through the perimeter with an old pair of scissors. The cast-off circle of blanket had remained on the floor right where he had thrown it, for several months now.

Books fell off his desk onto the floor, as if trying desperately to return by themselves to his expansive library shelves. They had been too long separated from their own kind. Notes were scattered here and there. Gary's latest note book and diary were open and a variety of pens lay about on the small rosewood desk, some working, some frozen with the wintry air that would not be kept out. The rest of the house became a shadowy ghost that he rarely awoke into life. He just didn't care anymore. However, from within this bleak desert of existence, words or word-pictures would erupt onto the page, revealing the inner workings of his anguished soul when at last Gary could no longer hold them back.

Edgar Peacock, his neighbour, came around as often as he could but, being a stunt man for the movie industry, he had to leave quickly when he was called to a set. It could happen at any time, with the high level of injuries involved. Ed was an adrenaline junkie with the requisite "brass balls" for the job.

When he did visit his neighbour they were on good terms but Gary did not communicate much. Ed simply recounted his latest hair-raising adventures as a movie double. The more dangerous they were, the more Gary seemed to cheer up; at least it seemed so to Ed. On his latest assignment he had to go down some scary rapids in Africa and he decided to tell Gary all about it.

"You know, Gazza," (neither of them knew when Ed started calling Gary, "Gazza", but both acquiesced easily into that familiarity), "the most dangerous parts of any rapids are not the rocks or the fast-flowing water. Did you know that?"

They were sitting down at the kitchen table. Ed had discovered to his amazement that there was food in the fridge and coffee beans in the freezer. "How fresh are these eggs, Gazza? The flour looks okay. How about I make us some breakfast, pancakes, and omelette, while you brew some coffee?" Gary in turn had shuffled around, grunting in assent until the rich smells of ground coffee and maple syrup filled the kitchen. Gary even managed to raise his eyes to meet Ed's when asked the question.

"No Ed, I did not know that. Is it anything like the danger of going down the drain when I empty the bath tub? Oh, if you are going to tell me that the water spirals down the drain differently in Africa to here, I will have to tell you, Ed, that you are full of shit! It might be the shit of African elephants, Ed, but shit is still shit!"

Ed had long been in the company of men, men with brass balls, and was quite used to masculine brusqueness bordering on aggression. He dealt with it all the time at work. More than this, though, Ed could hear inside Gary's depression something like Edvard Munch's scream, just beyond the edges of his pain-filled eyes.

"Gazza, the most dangerous part of the rapids is the turbulence. Turbulence, Gazza! Now listen!" Gary felt very disinclined to do anything else that day and in fact felt some relief from Ed's ebullience and vigour. It pulled him out of himself, if only for an hour or two, before he, once again, was claimed by the black dog.

"It happened to a buddy of mine, and he drowned." Gary immediately perked up a bit.

"He went over a small fall. We do it all the time in rapids, no problem. But he went down nose first. Again, no problem! You just roll out of it and pop back up to the surface. But, and here is the point, Gazza, there's turbulence at the bottom of the falls. Do you know what that is? I mean technically, not just "rough waters" but what really happens. It's all about vortices. You can get trapped there. The vortices can trap you and you can't get out. So you drown and nobody can help. You either pop out or you don't. Bloody hell, Gazza, you don't want to get caught in a vortex. My friend did and look what happened."

"What happened, Ed?" Gary's question had the sound of a faint echo as if he were talking in a cave. He had in fact subsided into his coffee cup and was gazing at the whorls of coffee grounds. They were like fingerprints, he thought, perhaps I could get a reading on my fate.

"What happened? Are you listening? He drowned! My buddy drowned!"

"No, I meant what happened to him in the vortex? Did he pop out or did he disappear?"

"Did he . . . , what? What are you going on about? He dived into the turbulence and died. O the body came out some time later. But it's random, you never know when. You can't control that once you are inside it."

"I mean, do you know what happened to him during that time *in* the vortex?"

Ed had been friends with Gary long enough now to cotton on to the fact that Gary was now cogitating and his questions were really in relation to some process that had been ignited in him during the conversation. So he didn't get offended and instead lapsed into silence as they enjoyed a second cup of coffee together.

After a time, Gary pulled a crumpled piece of paper out of his pocket and slid it across the table. Ed. suddenly felt he had passed some sort of test and was on the edge of entering a new level of intimacy with this man who seemed so broken. He gently unfolded it and read the poem that was scrawled there.

until i surrender

living a life of hopeful anticipation
but the foundation of the house was rotten
bursts of scattering activity
plunges into mindless blackness
edifice crumbles at last

clutching to possessions
thieves come in the night
room laid bare
grasp at career
guard dogs bare their teeth
no entry here

family and home
slowly debts
the weight of saturn
cast into lead

"That's as far as I got," said Gary, quietly. "Maybe there's more to be taken from me." Ed felt a chill run along his back but he said nothing. If there was one thing Ed had learned as stuntman it was how to recognize when he or another man was close to the edge.

"I'll drop in again," he promised. "I'm going to the Snake River Canyon in the USA tomorrow, you know, to where Evel Knieval tried his jump."

"The only way across is to go down," replied Gary enigmatically, toying absently with the crumpled poem.

* * *

That night, Gary had a dream. It was a dream of humility in which he was in the centre of a room and others lined the walls, watching. A young man presented a book to him—a red box with a red string running through it. This is his solution to the problem of cause and effect. "How long do you think I have been working on this problem?" he said, faintly mocking, "a good deal longer than you." I do not have the faintest idea of what he is showing me, Gary thought. He felt humiliated, knowing nothing, or near to it. The room erupted in chanting. More people go around the room, taking turns to chat about this or that existential problem. One man looking at Gary had tears of compassion for his plight. Gary was submitted to a barrage of knowledge that he know nothing about. It was an ordeal. He did not know what to do next and began to weep. All his own ideas, plans, purpose, were washed away in this ordeal. Now, the master was in the room too, and Gary was rendered mute, with nothing to say. The master got up and moved away and Gary simply followed him.

Gary woke up shocked. There IS more to be taken from me. I don't think I can stand it. I just don't understand what is happening. The more I try to know, the more I get taken away from me. Just before the blackness consumed him, he remembered some lines from Faust:

> 'Tis written: "in the beginning was the Word."
> Here am I baulked: who, now can help afford?
> The Word—impossible so high to rate it;
> And otherwise must I translate it.

If by the Spirit I am truly taught.

Then thus: "In the beginning was the Thought"

This first line let me weight completely,

Lest my impatient pen proceed to fleetly.

Is it the thought which works, creates, indeed?

"In the beginning was the Power," I read.

Yet as I write, a warning is suggested,

That I the sense may not have fairly tested.

The Spirit aids me: now I see the light!

"In the beginning was the Act," I write.

It was late that night and Gary was in the basement yet again, unable to sleep. His body was wracked with symptoms and he was in considerable pain. He had no idea who to turn to, where to get relief, even what to say that might help someone to help him. He felt an unbearable nameless conflict rise up and he thought he would explode.

"If only someone could tell me what this is! If only I had a dream to guide me, some image, a voice . . . !"

Nothing came. He was alone in an unbearable conflict. Blindly, in desperation, he reached out with his hands; no, it was more like his hands reached out all by themselves, carrying wisdom he did not know, and they found a piece of clay. All at once his conflict entered the clay. His hands pressed against each other with terrific force. To his own amazement, under this pressure, his hands, and the clay, began to turn. Slowly, slowly, a vortex formed between his hands. Forces of opposition entered a secret cooperation. His fingers channelled out grooves in the clay as the vortex kept forming itself.

He had found his way to the form that lay behind all phenomenal forms.

The vortex is the UR-Image!

This name simply presented itself as such to Gary as his hands continued their movement through the clay.

Only much later did he remember the ancient Indian symbol of creation pictured as Mount Meru turning under the oppositional forces of the gods and demons, each group pulling on the cosmic snake coiled around the mountain. The mountain begins to turn and a vortex in the cosmic ocean forms, out of which arise all phenomenal forms of the world.

Gary had arrived at a new beginning and his hands carried the wisdom of the future. Whatever he would create from that point probably would be a new form. Perhaps even a new art form.

Deeds, acts, come first, just as Faust said.

1999: ALLEN

Scholars are strange creatures. When they're faced with some new evidence they like to add one and one together and arrive at one and a half; then they spend years arguing about what happened to the other half. The half that's missing is the ability to watch and listen—to follow the evidence where it leads, no matter how unfamiliar.

Peter Kingsley

A**LLEN BENJAMIN WAS AN ARCHAEOLOGIST.** He was passionate about his discipline but his colleagues had long ago turned their backs on him. Although he knew his job as well as anyone else in the field, he had succeeded in alienating himself from academia by publically backing the work of Marija Gimbutas. Both Allen and Gimbutas were passionate about language and studied etymology and linguistics. Allen saw that language was the invisible thread that connected the various factual discoveries of archaeology and which located them in a specific time period, with a specific meaning.

He had made the fatal professional mistake of delivering a lecture at Harvard in support of Gimbutas' methodology which he called, after Owen Barfield, an application of the historical imagination. He compared this method with the usual one of deductive thinking by suggesting that only the historical imagination can open us up to the *meaning* of a group of artefacts and that this was Gimbutas' great contribution when she demonstrated how her investigations of the Neolithic period of Europe reveal a time whose meaning could best be described as matriarchal, a time governed by a woman-centred culture, peaceful and promoting economic equality, and a time of goddess worship.

In order to demonstrate her methodology to his colleagues, Allen produced some research of his own, the last, it turned out, to the Academy. He was subsequently "run out of town". He began by introducing Irish mythology, his specialty, to the group, with a series of slides showing the most well-known artefacts and symbols of pre-Christian Ireland. He said that he accepted the controversy whether a single Celtic culture ever existed. He was not seeking, like Gimbutas did, to weave a range of artefacts, folk lore, geography and other cultural findings into a coherent whole. That was not the issue today. He pointed the group to an enigma that existed in their discipline. It was the Celtic spiral. There was no consensus and little understanding of the meaning of the Celtic spiral.

Allen strongly suggested that the deductive method of science could never release the meaning of the spiral anymore that looking at bricks can tell us the meaning of a cathedral. We have to use another organ of truth. The imagination!

Already there were some disturbances occurring in the audience as people shuffled about. He hastily went on to define what he meant by imagination. He asked, "Look, how can we recognize the whole in the part, as in an art piece or play? For example, you can take almost any piece of a play and there recognize the whole, e. g., *Hamlet*. I am just proposing the organ of apprehension we use to do that. Furthermore, how do we apprehend spatial relations as expressive of *meaning* and how do we overcome the modern mind-body gulf such that we can perceive, in the object, the processes of mind at work? The organ of apprehension is the imagination and it is an organ of truth. This is why I value the work of Gimbutas so much but let me go on and demonstrate the method of historical imagination for you, here today."

Allen went to the next slide, which showed a picture of Newgrange.

"You see those spirals on the rock just below the cave mouth? I want to demonstrate to you today that, following the method of Gimbutas, we can approach the *meaning* of the spirals.

"As you are no doubt aware, Marija Gimbutas studied linguistics and etymology. I am going to start off the same way. I will begin with the word "conspire" which gained my interest through a dream. "O God!" he heard someone whisper in the back. "We know the dictionary meaning of the word but I was drawn by its *sound*: as I say the word I can hear my breath expel air softly. The sound of the word conveys soft speech, mostly breath *with* another—that's the 'con' prefix. Perhaps you were con-spiring there in the back," he joked. No response came forward, so he added, "well, I suppose preference for staying in the dark is quite in keeping with that particular activity." The silence was turning nasty and Allen hastily moved on.

"So, in keeping with this methodology, I turned to the dictionary in order to deepen my approach to the word and its, what shall I call it, sound-meaning? I found there the word 'spire', meaning to breathe, of course. No surprise there but 'spire' also has two other meanings: a single turn of a spiral and a movement of tapering, rising to a point, like a church spire. These three meanings, in their modern usage, are quite separate. Yet they are linked by the word, 'spire'. So, I may ask, what could breathing, spirals, and tapering to a point, have to do with one another. This little word work suggests that at some time in our past, they *did* have something to do with one another. In much the same way, wind and spirit no longer have anything to do with one another but at one time, as registered in language, they did, in the word *ruach*.

Now Allen was getting warmed to his task and failed to notice the slow leakage from the room. "Here is an example of what the method demands. As I was doing this word work, a memory was triggered and I always accept such intrusions as belonging to the research I am doing. It was a memory of the dreams I have had over the years involving vortices. In one such dream I see an ancient rock carving depicting human figures with spirals emanating from their mouths. To this day I cannot locate any outer reference but the memory remains with me. Even at that time I began to think there was a connection between spirals and speech, as the dream suggests, but could go no further, that is until now, many years later.

"I decided to dig more deeply into the etymology of the word 'spire' and found that a spire, as one turn of a spiral arises from *spira* which means 'to coil'. A coil is a connected series of spirals as in a coil of rope etc. 'Coil' comes from *colligere*, Latin for 'collect'. This makes sense as a coil, in collecting spires together, *becomes* a coil.

Then a surprise! And it is very important to trust these surprises. The word "collect" arises, as I said, from colligere and *this* word emerges, in turn, from the etymological root of *leg-*. Leg-, as well as meaning to collect or gather (from the Latin *legere*, from which one meaning of religion also is derived), has derivative meanings of 'to speak', or *logos*."

Allen, flushed with enthusiasm, lifted his face from his notes to engage the audience with his conclusion. "I had at last penetrated through the historical depths of language, to the forgotten psyche, the ancient past as reconstructed in the mind of modern consciousness—and an image was released! This little nest of word-meanings releases an image that includes a sacred gathering, speech, spirals and tapering to a point, as in a church steeple. I call such a sound-meaning the *UR-image*!"

Now for the *coup de grace*, he thought.

"Let me show you, once again, the slide of Newgrange. When I look again at these magnificent ruins I can now clearly perceive a mouth from which emanates a collection of spirallic forms, perhaps to those gathered below, radiating outward from the centre, like a sector of a circle. From the listener's viewpoint, I see a rising and tapering to a point where creative speech emanates from the high priest standing at the mouth of the cave.

"This method, my friends, suggests strongly that the priest is a mouthpiece of the cave's wisdom, emanating from its dark interior and becoming "material" through him, as he speaks to the crowd listening below. Do we see here in Newgrange and its mysterious spirals, the UR-image underlying the modern meaning of inspiration?"

Having turned away from the slide and its bright reflection, it took Allen a moment to readjust to the relative dimness of the auditorium. The slight increase in echoes began to alert him that all was not well and when he could see clearly he did not like what he saw. For this audience of distinguished archaeologists, there was no cave wisdom emanating from this particular mouthpiece at all. The room was almost empty and Allen Benjamin knew his professional life in the Academy was over.

He had backed the wrong horse.

*   *   *

"Is there such a thing as an archaeologist in private practice?"

It was now a year later and Allen was sitting with the only colleagues, now friends, who had stayed constant during his slow but inevitable "disbarment" from all academic life. He had placed the box of rejection slips from publishers across the world on the table for their perusal. Without regular and prolific articles in prestigious journals, funding had dried up and Allen's classes were depleted of students. He finally had resigned, was given a modest severance package, and let go.

With this slow bleed approach, the Academy can thus eliminate colleagues who hold an intellectually offensive position, while claiming, at the same time, an unassailable deniability.

Edgar Peacock was an international tour guide, highly successful, who took people on expeditions throughout the world. His marketing tool was a guarantee of the "thrill of your life", a claim that he could make since most of his tours were to out-of-the-way archaeological digs. He always found a way to bring excitement to his tours, with no small thanks to his friends Allen, Gary (Gazza) and Poesy Pond who often accompanied him. Allen provided the background knowledge, while Gary and Po' had an uncanny knack of "following their noses", leading small groups of hushed tourists away from the beaten track, down spiraling stairways, through ancient, twisting tunnels, getting lost but without losing the thread back to the safety of the tourist buses. Altogether it was a dynamic combination of talent and people had to book years in advance.

"Look," said Gary, "we've all been thinking about it. You are at the end of one career, Allen, that's all. I mean people these days go through not 3 or 4 jobs but 3 or 4 *careers* during their working lives. You all know that I went through my own depression a few years ago, which led to a complete reinvention of myself, really. I thought, no, was certain that I was headed for a career of teaching and psychotherapy, particularly in the field of the evolution of consciousness, which still fascinates me by the way. But the whole thing was undermined . . ."

"His mind went under," chortled Poesy who loved the play with words.

"Well, I remember you weren't in such a good condition either, when I met you," retorted Gary, with a smile.

"I tell you what, though," chimed in Ed, "it was my lucky encounter with you both that led to the explosion of *my* career."

Ed had, in a manner of speaking, rescued Gary and Poesy, helping them to return to ordinary life, in some small fashion, anyway. He had been on one of his tours in India, Dharamsala, to be exact. His group of tourists was happily wandering around the Tibetan monuments and shops so he took some time off to go up the hill to McLeod Gange, the actual location of the exiled Tibetan government. He found himself standing in front of a boy who was sitting on some broken stairs. The boy could have been any age between seven and thirteen. It was hard to tell with the level of malnourishment in this part of the world. He had a begging bowl on the next step down and this too, so far, was not unusual. Ed had seen such scenes all over the world. What held Ed to the spot was something that no Western country could conceive of, let alone condone. This boy, quite alone, it seemed, was casually caressing the cobra that was coiled around his arm. Ed had heard that sometimes these snakes were defanged and thus used to attract tourists but the apparition alone was enough to hold him fascinated.

He was roused from the spell by some equally strange appearances moving towards him from out of the forest nearby. First he saw an elephant and his mahout move towards a metre-high barbed wire fence. With the utmost delicacy, the elephant straddled the fence and then crossed it, ambling on down the grassy hill.

"There is no way he could see his hind legs," Edgar said to himself *sotto voce*. "How could he know?"

"He knows!" Someone's voice broke into his reveries. It took Edgar a minute to realize that this disembodied statement was, in fact, a response to his question.

Coming into focus now were two people. They were clearly Western, at least *he* was. She was less defined. She could have been Egyptian, or is that Nordic with a tan? It's her eyes, he decided. Almond shaped blue-violet eyes. Very ambiguous, but also very intriguing! They both wore dirty kaftans and showed other signs of being well-travelled—long dirty hair, beard, torn shoulder bags, worn-out sandals, and lean tanned bodies. Their arms were scraped and cut from excursions into the forest. Her arms also bore some tattoos—black spirals!

Ed took all this in quickly. His experience as a world-travelled guide had taught him to do a quick scan of those who approached and make an assessment of any possible danger to him or his charges who usually were staring innocently at some statue or building, sure targets for the local con-men. Having decided that this couple, although undeniably strange-looking, even by Ed's standards, was harmless, Ed then entered what was to be the strangest conversation he had ever had with any person, but one that opened up a new friendship and led to their present professional collaboration as well.

"What do you mean?" he asked.

"You know very well what he meant," she said with equal assurance.

"Ok. Let's pretend that I know what he . . . well, what is your name anyway, meant?"

"I am Gary, and she's Poesy, and you are Edgar Peacock."

Edgar suddenly felt a slight slippage occur. He turned to the boy and saw the cobra staring at him intently.

"Yes, you might well turn to Him," the amused Po' said," Not much else can help you now."

It was then that Edgar saw a tattoo on the man Allen. A small cobra was coiled up at his throat. It was black, too, like her, what was her name again, *Poetry*, spirals.

A feminine voice now intruded into Ed's racing thoughts. "Poesy, not 'poetry'! We are concerned with the *making*, not the *made*". Again, slight amusement hung in the air.

"What do you mean . . . ?" Ed began to realize that he was beginning to repeat himself. The slippage was getting worse.

"Don't worry, Ed," said Gary cheerfully. "You'll get used to it. She used to have that effect on me, too."

"I still do," Poesy reminded him. She then went over to the young boy and the cobra which still had its eyes fixed unwaveringly on Ed, who felt he needed to sit down.

"Well, my friend," she said, and Ed was not sure at all who she was talking to, "What do you think? Is he the one You had in mind to get us back?" She gently stroked the serpent's head. The cobra appeared to yawn, as snakes do when they need to rearticulate the jaw after consuming a meal. Edgar noticed that, notwithstanding his knowledge about beggary and the de-fanging of snakes, this particular one was fully equipped to deliver the death blow. He held his breath.

"Relax, Ed." This from Gary, quietly. "She is in conference, that's all."

Poesy began to hum, swaying slightly and the cobra moved with her head. The boy seemed quite at home with all this, smiling and holding out his hand for money from whoever was nearby. After a few moments, she gently withdrew. By this time Edgar was feeling quite faint. Gary reached into his shoulder bag and drew out a water bottle. He splashed some water on Edgar's face. "Come on," he said, 'It's time to go."

"Oh, OK," Edgar replied, wondering where his sudden acquiescence, or surrender really, had come from. "Where are we going?"

"Home of course," cried out Poesy who had joined them again, "But first we must find Allen."

"Who's Allen?" Ed asked, although he felt that it didn't really matter now. What mattered, although he could not fathom *why* it mattered, was his being with Gazza and Po'. Who? Where on earth did *those* names come from, he thought to himself?

"Ahh," laughed Gary. "He's getting there, Po'. He's getting there. It shouldn't take too long."

And now, the four friends were sitting around Allen's kitchen table. Po' dipped into the box of editorial rejection slips—pink slips they were called—and started to tear them up, or more precisely, she was tearing words out of the slips at random.

"Allen! Do this! Then rearrange the words any how!" The imperative in her voice was as *She Who Must Be Obeyed* and Allen complied without thinking. Ed looked on intently while Gary got up to make some coffee for them all. They lapsed into silence while Allen completed his task. Finally, they saw an arrangement of words on the table that read this way:

> At this time
> Unable to find
> Future regret
> Your endeavours
> Inform the future
> Your goals
> Match our needs
> Success

"Propitious indeed," whispered Po', "but there is warning and we must act now!"

"What do we have to do?" Allen was shaking and he grabbed the hot coffee Gary placed on the table. Ed had by this time given up asking Poesy and Gary useless questions. He simply followed the thread that they were divining somehow. Allen would get there too, he was sure. Much depended on his doing so.

"We must enter the vortex. Together! It is *kairos*! The right time! Or will be when we get there, but we must leave soon. Tonight!"

"Where, for god's sake," pleaded Allen. "Where is this vortex? And why must we enter it?"

"Why, at Newgrange of course," said Poesy gaily.

"What, are you mad? That's halfway across the world."

Even Edgar had trouble with that one. "It's a tourist trap now, Po', you know that. You can only get in with guided tours—mine for example. It'll take weeks to get a booking."

"We'll go there tonight," laughed Po'. She was in full swing now, joy lit her face, and Gary knew why. This was what she was born to do. She was in her element.

With Allen's string of failures and rejections still burning his heart, he felt he couldn't stand this nonsense. "By what possible means, by what possible fucking *way*, could we get to Newgrange and this fucking vortex that we are supposed to enter? Is this another one of your *thrills*, Edgar?"

Completely unfazed by Allen's coffee-spilling outburst, Po' answered him directly and soberly, all laughter gone now. He could not therefore mistake *her* intent.

"We will go by the way of *phōlarchos*," she said matter of factly.

1976: PO'

. . . Either I am losing my mind—"

"Now, now, Miss—"

"—or the world has changed. It is as if, as if I have gone into some other place, alien and frightening, and I am trapped there and unable to get out."

I sit for a time wrapped in my own silence, fearful of emerging. I have had, after all, no experience dealing with the deranged. But finally pity makes me speak. "You did, though. You did, my dear Miss Tangerie, so it cannot be as bad as all that."

"I did what?"

"Get back out. Clearly you managed to do so."

"Why can't you understand?" she cries. "I did not get out. I am still trapped here."

Stephen Marlowe

"I DON'T UNDERSTAND A WORD she is saying," said the sergeant.

"Did she do any damage to any property, or harm anyone?"

"No Sir! But she was half-naked, and I don't mind telling you she's got quite the bod . . ."

"That will do, Sarge. Enough of that! Get her some clothes, will you? And Sarge . . ."

"Yes Sir?"

"Take Constable Jones along with you."

"Yes Sir. Of course, Sir"

"This is a weird one, Jones. You've never seen anything like this." The sergeant had found a gown from the Red Cross and gave it to Jones. "You go into the room and make her put this on," he said. "I'll be in after that."

Jones entered the holding cell and saw a slender woman with wild dark hair. Her torn dress, if you could call it that by now, revealed a tattoo on her arm, a black spiral. But it was her eyes that arrested Jones' attention. Blue-violet orbs looked back at her, unblinking. No not quite, she thought. Not "looked at" but "looked *into*". They seemed slightly out of focus and Jones suddenly felt naked, or better, transparent to those eyes. She felt she could not hide anything nor especially, did she want to. The other oddity about her eyes was their slight erratic movements, as if the young woman could not quite focus on her.

That tattoo will help with the identification, thought Jones, recovering herself somewhat. She immediately felt a sisterly pity for this fallen woman, who, she was sure, was some sort of prostitute, fallen on hard times. But for the grace of god go I, she thought.

"Here put this on. It's warmer than what you have. What's your name?"

The young woman opened her mouth to reply and the strangest thing happened. Jones later tried to recount the experience to her husband and friends but had to give it up. It was too hard. She suddenly felt a deep longing in her soul. Jones was not one for sentimentality. She had not, up to now, given much thought to even having a soul. In this way Jones was thoroughly modern. She simply knew how to make goals and attain them. But now she *longed* . . . She longed for something unnameable. She then swore she could hear the ocean, or rather, a bell-like sound, or was it a moan? Whales! That was it! A far-off sound of whales! But they are crying, moaning, or is that *my* moaning. Oh, the grief, I can't stand it. My heart is breaking. Whaling! Wailing?! O no, we cannot go on this way. It's hurting me. I can't bear it . . ."

"Jones! Jones, are you done? Is she dressed? I'm coming in."

Thoroughly disoriented, Jones stood up. How long have I been sitting down next to this woman? She hastily began to arrange her hair, stammering, "I've been interviewing her, Sergeant. It appears she comes from the sea." What did I just say? My god, I am going to get roasted for this.

"From the seaside, you say? Well, what suburb might that be, Miss?" The sergeant was a man of the facts, just gimme the facts, and thus missed almost the entirety of Jones' implicit communication, which, perhaps, accounts for his remaining a sergeant after thirty years on the job.

The woman remained silent, with just the hint of a smile on her lips, disarming the sergeant before he could reach for the familiar weapons of aggression that he used in his interrogations. "Jones, you take care of this and get the report to me by tomorrow, would you?" He left the room, banging his head on the door on the way out. This gaffe ignited a sudden, inexplicable rage, silently inflaming his face momentarily before he could bring it under control. He turned and closed the door with a studied calmness, glancing momentarily at Jones to make sure there was no sign of insubordination threatening to destroy all law and order. He wasn't sure, as he stormed down the linoleum hallway, whether, inside the comforting sound of his boots and their familiar and steadying military march, he had heard another sound, of bells, or was it laughter, trailing behind him.

*　　*　　*

"What will we do with her? She hasn't officially been diagnosed yet and should be referred here by the hospital."

"Well, Dr. Peacock. This really is my last resort. The sergeant told Jones to get rid of her and so she palmed her off on to me. You know how big my case-load is. I am the only social worker in the area and I just haven't got the time for this. Take her for a few days. You've got a spare room, at least I think so, since, well, you know, since Peter off'd himself."

It was still a sore point. Chiron House was walking on a tightrope as it is. Peacock hadn't needed a publicized suicide to remind "the establishment" of the dangerous stupidity of putting a bunch of schizophrenic patients together in the one residential home and helping them through their illness without prescribed medication. Using volunteer staff simply made the matter worse and having police knock on the door at all hours because neighbours complained about the periodic roars, wails, and yes, sometimes, violence, that broke out was about the last straw for the Board of Mental Health. Peacock, as the resident psychiatrist, was legally responsible for it all and the shit would rain down on him first and foremost. It probably was only a matter of time . . .

Peacock stood quietly as the memories of last week's nightmare had their play with him, and took in this oddly dressed young woman who gazed back, totally unafraid and not the least bit threatening. But she was strange that's for sure. And her eyes are nervous, no, just slightly erratic. That's interesting!

Well, you asked for this, he reminded himself. You thought the system would be too boring. You believed it wasn't helping anybody. You had to read Szasz and Laing and get all fired up. You wanted the excitement, the thrill of the unknown, didn't you? So you had to start up this place, with little funding for god's sake! Well, buddy, you got it! Here it is!

He had been looking at the young woman all this time, who gazed back. His reveries, which must have registered as momentary pained flickers across his face, were interrupted by a peal of laughter. Peacock was shocked "into the moment" as his colleagues liked to say.

"She likes to do that," said Julie. "I don't know what to make of it."

"Oh, bring her in. Gazza can set up her room. Maybe *he* knows something. He's always researching the schizophrenias. This could be a version of hebephrenia." Peacock regretted speaking that last thought out aloud. He actually hated diagnostic categories and he hated talking about people that way, especially when they were right there. But he was tired, very tired. The previous week had been hell.

It had started when Peter, psychotic as the best of them, said he wanted to go to hospital and knew how to do it. He was going to shove his fist through a window. His body moved like an automaton, there was so much repressed emotion—rage, terror, and panic in his body. His limbs looked as though they were joined by pins. Edgar and Gary, another professional staff member, saw him move towards the window and jumped on him, determined not to have the police come this night, since they had already visited the previous evening. His strength was enormous and they could not hold him. When he reached for the nearest carving knife, they backed off. He ran from the room, slipped, and fatally stabbed himself. No one believed that story for a moment, not even Julie the social worker. No, it became a suicide very quickly, fed by the various vested interests in having the place shut down.

The house was quiet as Julie handed her charge over to Gary who was a psychiatrist-in-training, and a volunteer at Chiron. He was there to learn all he could about psychosis. He was working on the theory that madness and creativity were related somehow. He just had to do the research, write it up and he would be admitted to the College. He was lucky enough to find a patient here who could give him the data he needed: Al. Neither Gary nor Edgar could determine his condition. He had presented with some of the symptoms of schizophrenia, hearing voices, seeming loss of touch with ordinary reality, etc., and his art work clearly had features that would alarm the medical profession for sure. But what intrigued Gary most of all about Al was the *volume* of artistic output. They had given him a shed out the back to work in and were hard pressed to provide him with enough materials he needed to express . . .

Express *what*? Well, what *would* you call it, mused Gary, as he absent-mindedly guided the young deranged woman (well she *looked* deranged, but he wasn't really paying attention, he was still trying to work Allen out) to her room. Edgar and Julie were left arguing, as usual, about the exact nature of Peter's demise, and Edgar was getting heated. Julie was certain that it was suicide even though Edgar had been there and seen it all and she hadn't. It was preposterous but there it was. He could do nothing about it.

As Gary led the young woman down the long dark hall, it seemed to him that the arguing voices were getting fainter, but disproportionately to the actual distance they had gone. He felt he was in a tunnel, just he and . . . what was her name, anyway? He looked back and into her blue-violet eyes and immediately felt a slight vertigo. Depth opened up and for a moment he thought he heard a whale song, or was it bells? He felt a stab of fear. He turned away and they were at her bedroom door. The moment had passed.

*   *   *

"That was the best thing you could have done, Gazza!"

"I agree. It was a stroke of genius," Gary admitted immodestly. They were in the kitchen, just the two of them for once. With five volunteer staff and eight patients at any one time, the kitchen and bathroom were rarely unoccupied. But, it *was* the "morning after" and they knew they could relax for a few days. Nothing much would happen.

This was one of the great clinical discoveries that they had made since Chiron had got underway. A house full of schizophrenics had its own life and they were all subject to its breathing cycles, staff and patients alike. And they had all just emerged from the exhalation phase in which psychotic outburst ignited psychotic outburst. It went on for days. One woman, Pam, thoroughly paranoid, with unassailable delusions of reference, had bought herself a galah and perched him on her shoulder as she ranted and raved throughout the house. She commandeered the living room and soon the bird began to imitate her screeching accusations that ripped through the house. No one wanted to go in and stop it. When Ed looked in briefly he saw her dancing wildly in a white shift while the galah, its crest in full display stretched its equally white wings out full-length and shrieked at him, warning him away. It wasn't hard to oblige.

Pam's decompensation set Ted off at around 2am. There was no sleeping during these times, and Gary had to sit with him while he descended into terrified suicidal ideation, begging Gary to take him to the ward. Gary complied with this request. He had to as it was part of the condition for setting Chiron up in the first place—patients must be free to return to hospital. Two other patients decided this was the best time to explore their homosexual longing for each other and so, as well as the shrieks and wails of Pam and bird, everyone could hear groans and a mad squeaking as the old spring-loaded bed started to give way under the impact of two rather large men-at-work. A few other patients simply escaped into the night down to the corner all-night coffee shop, where one was later arrested for sexually relieving himself behind a bush nearby. Bruce was harmless, Edgar knew this. Bruce had told Edgar that when he masturbated he saw his mommy giving him milk, and it was good. Two other night-time volunteers spent three hours "working with" a patient, Jacque, who, for all intents and purposes, dressed like the devil. He had a well-worked out and stable delusional system that involved life on other planets. It had also flared up during the night and so they were held spell-bound in his room as he proceeded to enlighten them about how things really worked around here. At no point during Jacque's stay at Chiron, could any of the staff be sure whether he was actually violent or just looked that way, in the way that Dracula looks violent. Both volunteers therefore just decided to ride it out until he finally fell asleep.

So this was the "morning after"! The storm had spent itself and everyone was becalmed. Someone had managed to rescue the galah and clean up the droppings that festooned chairs and carpet. Pam was draped unconscious on the couch with a smile on her face. Her slip was over her head so it seemed that someone had braved the fury of the storm enough to enter and sow a seed or two for the future. Probably old Barry, Edgar thought. He was a chronic schizophrenic with a heavily sexualized imagination coupled with maternal yearnings, like Bruce. He also was rather harmless. He would never force himself on any one since he was so child-like and simple. No, Pam probably grabbed and plundered *him*, as she had done in the past.

Gary made some coffee for them both, taking out his secret stash of real coffee, coffee that he had ground from the bean. The patients seemed satisfied with instant coffee and they had a meagre budget anyway. The bitter, aromatic smell filled the kitchen space and they both felt themselves relaxing a bit.

"Where did they go, do you know, during all this?"

"Who?" Gary was immersed in his coffee mug savouring the brew. "O yes, Al and, what *is* her name anyway?"

"We're calling her Po," said Ed. "Al suggested it to me, after your brilliant stroke of introducing them to each other."

They had become inseparable and since they were adults, no one objected to Al moving into Po's bedroom. They divided their time between her bed and his "art studio" out the back, and, by all measures, were cooking up quite a storm together.

"Yeh, I just had a feeling about her. I don't think she is hebephrenic at all, Eddie. And, I am beginning to believe Al is quite with it, too. I don't think we have categories for those two, ya know. How can I put it? This is not a clinical judgement. I don't want you to hold me to this. And I am not going to put this in my research findings at all. I can't, it's too weird."

"I'm with you so far, Gaz. I am beginning to have similar doubts. So tell me your non-professional opinion. What going on with these two?"

"Well, it's only my interest in the relationship between madness and the creative spirit that has opened me up to these thoughts and perceptions at all, Ed. I have learned that the imagination is not only a storehouse for memory or sense-based images. It's also an organ for truth, properly understood. You and I know that the imagination today is regarded by our profession as, at best, a place of fiction, not reality. We are taught not to pay any attention to the content of psychosis but to normalize the patient as much as possible, which is why psychiatric wards are designed to look like hotels. It's absurd but there we are."

"Yup, agreed," said Edgar.

"So, even with all this prejudice in our profession, and beyond, I have begun training myself to pay attention to what my imagination brings me in relation to perceiving the world. So, with Al and, what is it, Po', I "saw" that they both seem to be coming into focus, more as each day passes here. This is difficult but I had an experience when I first met Po', walking down the hall. It was like another dimension of reality was appearing and we were stepping into it together. I felt she knew this was happening. Then it was gone. But since that time, I began to see Al differently, like he too was somewhere else and was struggling, through the only means available, his art work, to come into focus. It's like they are trying to *get* here, whatever the hell that means."

They were quiet again. The steam from the coffee rose lazily upward until tiny vortices formed and dissipated, breaking the smooth stream into unpredictable turbulence. Gary had studied such matters and muttered, "can you see how the turbulence is unpredictable and yet the vortices, once formed, seem stable for a time?"

Edgar was still thinking about Gary's remarkable, if highly unorthodox, perceptions of Al and the young woman, Po, or Po' as he had written in her case notes. How the hell would I know it was Po spelled with an apostrophe anyway, he thought? She can't write . . . but his thoughts were interrupted by Gary's newest observations so Edgar found himself staring at the rising steam, too. "Yes, I see what you mean. And they interact with one another, too, before they dissipate."

"The simplest systems, like this streaming air flow seem to have this inbuilt chaos that it can break into at any time, quite unpredictably."

"Now that's interesting," said Edgar. "I remember now that chaos theory has something to say about schizophrenia. You know, how their eyes move erratically around an object, unable to stabilize or focus. Nobody knows why but it could have something to do with a simple system breaking into turbulence." As they ruminated together, they could both feel something gathering, like disparate pieces of a puzzle, swirling in turbulence and forming a vortex that slowly came into focus. They looked at each other. Allen and Po'! Together they rose from the table, Edgar spilling his coffee on the floor, and they rushed outside to the shed that doubled as Allen's "art studio".

"Have you ever been inside?" asked Gary. "No, I wanted to give him privacy. I think they are both there now. Have you?" "No, likewise. He just asks for more paint, or paper and I order it for him. I have only seen some early samples he showed me. But that was some time ago now." As they approached the shed, they both could feel what only could be described as a pressure wave building. It was like walking through a viscous liquid. By the time they reached the door, it was quite strong and each man had to *will* his way forward.

At the periphery of his vision, Gary detected a faint blue-violet light pervading the air, extending from the shed outwards. He knocked on the door. It was partially ajar so both men entered.

In the centre of the floor rose a small blue-black vortex. It was winding erratically here and there, dissipating, forming again, but growing increasingly more stable.

"He's done it," said Po', "and you have arrived just in time. We must go."

She was sitting on the floor gazing at the vortex. Her blue-violet eyes were steady now, all signs of wavering were gone, and she could speak!

Allen also seemed strangely at peace. He was lying on the small bed. "It took some work to get her here. I wasn't sure . . . I couldn't remember . . . I had to paint it at first, to remember the image. Then I knew I had to generate the image and stabilize it. The more I could do that the more Po' came into focus, along with the vortex. I couldn't understand what she was saying—there was too much turbulence. I needed to paint caves, lairs, animals lying in caves. She kept saying something over and over, until I got it—*phōlarchos*! That was it! Phōlarchos! And I remembered: *that's* the way back!"

Gary and Edgar looked at the walls and ceiling of the little shed. They were covered with paintings of animals, caves, scenes of interpenetrating figures, at all orientations. The little rosewood desk that Edgar had given to Al some time ago was now decorated with paintings of vortices and spirals.

Gary had a startling feeling of recognition.

"My god, this is like the caves in France—at Lascaux!"

"Yes," echoed Edgar in amazement, "like Lascaux."

"It's time," sang Po', radiant in the intensifying blue-violet light.

"Lie down," ordered Allen, who was now invested with a strange authority. Edgar and Gary complied. "No, don't cross your legs, just drop on the ground. Collapse! Let yourself go. Nothing fancy!"

Po' had curled up like small animal and Allen, too, just crumbled where he stood. He now concentrated all his will on the vortex which was strong and stable, holding it steady. He had to, until the others had sufficiently surrendered. Po' was there already but he could see that Gazza was struggling to comprehend what was happening. Edgar, on the other hand was indulging his excitement again. The thrill-seeker, sighed Allen. He had to help them deeper into the trance-state.

"Gazza! Let your hands do the work. Pay attention to your hands."

Gary looked at his hands and found to his amazement that they had coiled around each other. A faint inexplicable memory appeared. Hands, moving through clay, terrible torment . . . Caught thus by surprise, he suddenly dropped.

"That's it. Now Edgar, ride the wave. That's it, go with it. Let it take you down, down. No need to be afraid of those depths. It's just *depth*. Like Po's eyes . . ." Edgar saw Po's eyes swelling up in front of him, enormous, Love filled his heart, and a blue-violet light spread out before him. He was no longer afraid. My god, how long have I been afraid of those depths, he thought, just before he plummeted down into the black vortex that now surrounded and permeated them all.

1965: RETURN AND ON

A phōleos is a lair where animals hide, a den. Often it's a cave . . . It's a place where animals go into retreat: where they lie motionless, absolutely still, hardly breathing.

Phōlarchos are healers. They would lie down in an enclosed space. Often it was a cave. And either they'd fall asleep and have a dream or they'd enter a state described as neither sleep nor waking—and eventually they'd have a vision.

Peter Kingsley

IT WAS BLACK, VERY QUIET, and there was strange smell that assailed Edgar's nose. He decided to stay very still until he knew where he was and what was going on. His heart was pounding and he thought it would leap out of his chest. It was a similar feeling to when he wiped out on a big break. The wave would push him down, down and he would begin to panic but knew he mustn't, that he must get back to the surface, he must stay calm. What is that stench?

His eyes slowly adjusted to the light, dim though it was. It was less dark over there. And now he could see some outlines nearby, motionless. A searing light suddenly appeared from the blackness. He averted his eyes in instant pain. It increased exponentially and a band of light appeared on the . . . it's sand, a sandy floor. As his eyes accustomed to the brilliance, he could see a cup, upside down inside a giant mouth, spilling liquid light down on him. Now there was a stirring in the sand that sent shockwaves of fright through him. He could see well enough that it was alive, and had four legs. He froze.

The dingo had been desperately ill. The rabbit that it caught on the side of the road had been poisoned and so now was the dog. So it did what many animals do. It found its way to its lair, vomited up the meal, and then curled up in a ball, to live or to die, as nature saw fit. Three days passed. Now, in the new moon, the crisis had passed and the dingo was to live a while longer. It uncurled slowly, stretched its hind legs out and rose slowly, a little wobbly. The ascending moon cast the Australian bush into sharp relief. The mouth of the cave held the moon briefly in its teeth before releasing it to continue on its orbit and sinking back into semi-darkness.

He was aware but unconcerned with the four unfamiliar forms that lay supine on the sandy cave floor. He quietly moved over to the where the interesting odour was, his last meal, and sniffed it. Experience warned him against eating it again and he moved over to the edge of the cave, marked it with his scent, and then trotted out into the bush, melting into the darkness.

By now Edgar could see fairly well and recognized the human outlines next to him. Po' was the next to waken, moaning softly. This stirred, in turn, Gary and then Allen, and all four friends slowly gathered their wits enough to ask the usual questions, where am I, how did I get here, I don't know, is everybody ok, what time is it, how long have we been here, what's that terrible smell, etc. They huddled together in the cold, speaking in low whispers, and together decided to wait right where they were until daybreak. They knew how easy it is to get lost in the Australian bush. There were some hours before the false dawn and Gary asked, "Do you remember anything, anything at all?"

Po' exclaimed, "the vortex! Of course!"

"You mean that wretched dust devil that Ed the bloody adventurer sucked us all into. What happened anyway . . . ?"

"No, no, the vortex! We arrived there. We found our way to the spiralled rock. We entered the tunnel, the chamber. Don't you remember?"

"Yes, yes," said Allen. "It was very dark but with a shaft of moon light at the end, the very end. We reached it and found the triple spiral and the . . ."

"The black vortex," chimed in Gary.

"But I've never been to such a place," said Edgar. "How could I remember it? This is crazy."

They fell into silence once again and waited, as we once probably waited millennia ago, not knowing, just waiting, feeling the comfort that only warm bodies can bring, until the first rays of sun broke into the cave and ended their long vigil.

*   *   *

It took some time to deal with anxious and fretting parents and nosy school chums. During that long night the Three Musketeers, as Allen like to play, decided not to mention the dust devil but to simply say that they had got lost in the bush due to one of Edgar's silly thrill-seeking games. It was the easy way out since most people seek the certainty of the easy explanation and are keen to overlook the little details that would cast doubt on the account given, details such as a bicycle and three back packs lying in the middle of the road. So, after a time, everything returned to normal and the four friends—they were quite definitely friends now—were left to their own devices.

They agreed to meet regularly after school at Allen's home since his parents did not return from work until around six. That gave them a few hours to try to organize their thoughts and discuss the whole matter. They sat around Allen's kitchen table and tried to pool their memories into a coherent story, but try as they might it would not congeal. Instead they each were left only with fragments, thoughts, images, strange words, and dream images. Nothing was the same for any of them. It seemed to Edgar that they were remembering what they had not yet done but how could that be? It was impossible. The fragments that they could remember remained as inexplicable as they were *alive.* They acted as an engine, pushing the four forward into their lives.

Edgar for example had strong feelings of wanting to travel, to explore the unknown. There were places he needed to see, to explore. He heard of the burgeoning science of the brain and its interest in alternate states of consciousness. Some neuroscientists and Buddhist monks were working together to explore the deeper reaches of the mind while others were studying dream-states, such as the well-known hypnogogic state. Edgar realized that his enthusiasm for experience could include travel of *inner* worlds and he eagerly entered a dual career in medicine and psychology, riding, as it were, the new wave of discoveries in the mind-brain enigma that still baffled modern science.

Gary was besieged by thoughts that he could not associate to any known ideas he had learned at school or elsewhere, for that matter. He gained a passion for knowledge. He had heard about the new mathematics—chaos theory and its central question of chaos, turbulence, strange attractors, and boundary conditions. He was fascinated by the close connection between turbulence and vortices. It was Po' who showed him fractal art, which "clinched the deal" for him—and yes, he did pass that trope on to Allen who dutifully wrote it down in his growing collection of quotations, a collection that he hoped one day would become a book—a book of quotations, no commentary, no citations, just the quotes. When Gary asked him why, he could only say that he was following a thread that would reveal itself to him one day.

Allen continued to love Po' although their paths separated for many years. She had sensed that the depth of his love for her could drown him unless he also developed his intellectual side. His soul needed drying out, she concluded. Indeed Allen began to study mythology, depth psychology, and symbolism. It was the perfect match for his poetic and intuitive mind. He was particularly gripped by the ancient Greeks' mediation practices at the time of Parmenides as well as the Asclepian incubation techniques of dreaming and healing.

Po', in turn, wandered. She was proficient in several languages and became a poet of some note. Even her ordinary speech was poetic in the sense that others often felt that they were being *engendered* by her words and thus gave birth to new thoughts, and images. Artists sought her out to be their muse but she avoided this trap, preferring to remain independent and thus relatively unseen, although her words were heard quite frequently, uncited, as the lyrics of a new song that made the hit parade.

Although their paths were on different trajectories, they found from time to time that they would wind back together for short periods. Once, when they thus came together, Gary fondly imagined that a strange attractor was governing the seemingly random paths they were on. When no one mocked him or dismissed the thought, he was emboldened to go on with this theory.

"The thing about the strange attractor," he said, "is that it is a *form* that is a kind of boundedness or order to what seems to be observably chaotic behaviour of a system. It is not a phenomenon. We can't see a strange attractor. What we see, for example in our own lives, are paths that seem determined by contingency, going this way and then that and apparently meeting at random every few years. Yet our meetings seem very meaningful to me, and, I think, you too."

All heads nodded in assent to this.

He went on. "A strange attractor technically occurs in a mathematical space, called *phase space*, a map of all the possibilities of a system, once reduced to its smallest number of independent variables, such as position, velocity, time etc. The invention of the computer made phase space "visible" to us because only the computer could compute the billions of possibilities of a non-linear dynamic system in a reasonable time. Random plots scattered over the screen, slowly give way to the emergence of a strange, ghostly and often very beautiful shape.

The more points that are plotted the more the shape comes into focus. Although the system never loses its chaotic nature, it also becomes clear that the system stays with some bounds. For example there are areas that no point ever goes, indicating that the system never has these particular co-ordinates or values. Or, there are values that lie far apart at times yet come together unpredictably at other times, all governed by the shape of the strange attractor—like we do. Are you with me on this?"

Not only were they with him but, to his surprise, could contribute to the discussion in those very terms.

Edgar addressed the enormous interest in brain research with unstable states that can be described by chaos theory—heart arrhythmia, the erratic eye movements of schizophrenia, certain epileptic seizures, and so on. Allen had been fascinated by fractal art for some time and told them how our minds now had to somehow embrace ideas such as an infinite line within a finite area, dimension that was non-integer, shapes that were self-similar over scale and yet non-repeatable, meaning they cannot be described by deterministic equations and so on.

Po' took them all into the most mysterious aspect of all, the question of turbulence. She took up Gary's idea of the strange attractor:

"As you know turbulence involves vortices, coming and going, stretching, interacting, repelling, stable, and then dissipating without any predictability. We can see these vortices quite easily, for example, with wind tunnels and smoke streams. As observable phenomena, they seem to me to be also symbolic i.e. they also seem to me to be speaking to us about how the mind may work. I have not read about a vortex being an attractor for a chaotic system except for the rotating torus which is an attractor for a simpler non-linear dynamical system. Vortices are more regarded in terms of the observable aspects of turbulence which may or may not have a strange attractor, you know, one of those beautiful and weird geometrical shapes in phase space that Gazza talks about.

"But I am thinking somewhat differently about vortices of late," she went on. "They seem to me to be the first or *original* forms emerging from within chaos, sort of a form of forms, and therefore not in itself phenomenal but that original 'form' that gives rise to *all* phenomenal form. I call it the UR-image!"

Both Edgar and Gary broke in excitedly at this point. Po's speech always had this germinating effect on others, somehow generating images or forms in their minds, which, in their subsequent utterances, became speech.

Edgar won the good-natured tussle with Gary and went on. "There is much evidence in nature of finished forms that to us look like the solid residue of a vortex at work. Take the spirallic form of the human heart for example. It looks like it was formed by an invisible vortex."

"Yes," interrupted Gary, unable to contain himself any longer, "and there is that ancient Indian myth of creation where a vortex, itself non-phenomenal, gives rise to all forms of life."

"When you think about it," pondered Edgar, "our little dust devil, all those years ago, has had that effect on us. We each seemed to gain access to, what shall I call it, alternative lives, possible futures, where things are achieved, done, and which we now seem to be, as odd as it sounds, remembering, as they become *our* future, over time. That's weird!'

"Not so weird, my friends," sang Poesy Pond. "Others have been there too."

She and Allen flawlessly broke into poetic speech, alternating in turn. First Allen quoted Rilke:

> The future enters us
> In order to transform itself
> Long before it happens

Then, Po' intoned:

"Two worlds collide—such generative violence—and there is a becoming. 'Life at the core is steel on stone' from which emerges the new form. What we call art is a palpable echo of two galaxies slowly winding through each other over millennia tearing their cells apart with the cosmic force of love yet holding their integrity with spirallic majesty, forever able to carry the memory of that great encounter."

Finally they alternated stanzas:

crowd gathers
centering young woman
struggling to walk

tune of derision mockery
only a cane to help her
legs so long and slender
curving stretching down
feet ending
strangely bending toes

no one knows her
where does she come from?
dark hair damply hanging
long shoulder sloping

brave souls addressing
song breathing from her lips
brave souls retreating

crowd offers more distant observations

such strange musical notes
escaping her mouth

moved to silence at first
distant memory stirring
bells water
tinkling against stone
tones
uncanny echoes blue depths
long forgotten by mankind.

but among men
this beautiful silence of possibilities
so quickly filling
with known safety of fear

rock found
passing hand to hand
air suddenly cracking tight
rope pulled hard.

i am pulled too
but towards her
in that moment i see

eyes blue-gray reflections
sky upon water
hair windswept waves
legs strong lean
awkward hurting
toes not deformed at all
transparent skin webs
more used to a friendlier touch
than what hard ground can offer

voice echoing another world

we once knew

now left far behind

love welling in my heart

music filling

penetrating

awakening dormant knowing

gentle tinkling sea bells,

deep moans of leviathan

forming words within me

emerging from deep immersion in her

seeing rock raised to throw

stepping forward

crowd giving way

wave parting

stop! can't you see?

she is not crippled

she is a mermaid a mermaid a mermaid

she is not seeking alms or favours

she is seeking . . . us

listen to her

listen

i have come! i have come! i have come!

greetings! i have come!

2025: ALLEN'S BOOK OF QUOTATIONS

"I shall then have no more friends," said the young man."

Alas! nothing but bitter recollections."

And he let his head sink upon his hands, while two large tears rolled down his cheeks.

"You are young," replied Athos; "and your bitter recollections have time to change themselves into sweet remembrances."

Alexandre Dumas

MY FRIENDS ARE ALL GONE now. Edgar developed a brain cancer, which has its irony, given his passion for research into consciousness and the brain. He became the subject of his own research until he could no longer communicate his experiences to others. Although he never denied the biological basis of mind, he demonstrated to others his conviction that consciousness or soul has its own reality. Right at the end, his brain had been eaten away and there was literally nothing left with which to communicate. Ed was comatose and all that was left was to disconnect him. But right then, to everyone's shock he woke up, alert, and said his goodbyes. Anatomically he did the impossible. It must have been his last thrill ride, before he expired.

Gary strangely enough also died from a brain disease. In his case, meningitis invaded his brain tissue through the nose. The manner of his death was also very unusual. He began to have visions and even wrote some "death poetry", which he claimed, showed the way. Only Po' understood what he meant. She had visited him on his death bed, after many years away from us, and he told his last dreams and visions to her. For some reason she kept her counsel and once again disappeared from our, well no, *my* life now, for some years.

Gary had collaborated with Ed for many years, and together they made good ground in understanding brain processes through the lens of chaos theory, Gary's specialty. But he also branched into new areas of research with the problem of turbulence and the role that vortices play in it. He and I also engaged in some research together. He came to accept the correlative relationship between consciousness and world through my work on the evolution of consciousness. So it wasn't hard, in the end, to show him how turbulence and the forming of vortices, their interactions and so on were our perceptions, in the world, of deep unconscious processes of the mind at work. We are seeing what in fact we are.

I have never forgotten the vortex and I never forgot Po'. Although we had, as they say, "meaningful relationships" (Gazza would surely laugh at that tired cliché), we never married. We were all in love with Po', each in his own way. I kept hearing signs of her, in song or poem played over the airwaves. O yes, I could always recognize her voice.

After our emergence from the vortex, we each had been left with fragments of memory which presented themselves as possible futures. I simply could not understand how I could remember something that had not happened yet. Yet these fragments continued to work on us and our lives unfolded accordingly, in unexpected ways, but meaningfully so.

One of the ways I honored this process was by collecting quotes that I came across, over the years. They were fragments that mattered to me though I did not know why at the time. I only collected those quotes that found their way to me in moments of great need, when I needed support in the form of words. They sustained me by showing fragments of the meaning of what I was going through, similar to what others had also discovered and expressed. In this way I felt mentored by them, taken deeper into the mystery that was unfolding from within my passion. They were somehow related to the possible futures that the vortex showed us.

During this time of "gathering" I came across a remarkable man by the name of Walter Benjamin—yes, we share the same name! He had written some astonishing essays and what gave them their brilliance was his method! In the words of philosopher Hannah Arendt who did so much to bring his work forward into the public domain (and here is another one of my quotes):

> . . . [Benjamin] was concerned with the correlation between a street scene, a speculation on the stock exchange, a poem, a thought, with the hidden line which holds them together and enables the historian or philologist to recognize they must be placed in the same time period . . .

Walter Benjamin understood that, within the fragments of modern life, an underlying form may be discerned as the hidden thread that connects the fragments—a form that can begin to shape the future. I began to call this form the *UR-image*, as my beloved Po' had taught me.

Many years later I had a dream that explicitly linked my work to Walter's:

> A kindly blue-collar worker finds a copy of Walter Benjamin's third book for me. I want it but he says it costs $350. I try to find ways to negotiate the price. I go to another book store to see if they have it. I am driving and pull over quickly at a gas station as three people call me to show me a small book by WB. It shows beautiful illustrations along with his quotes. I want to have that one, too . . .

Following this dream, I pulled out my old copy of Benjamin's essays and was astonished to read that his greatest ambition was to create a book consisting entirely of quotations. i.e., no commentary necessary! The fragments themselves would express the hidden thread that unites them and places them in the same time period. As far as I knew, Walter never did create this book, yet the dream shows a completed book of quotations by Walter Benjamin.

Now, at seventy-five years old, I believe I may have enough quotes to begin my own book of quotations. Like my namesake's, it will be a book without commentary and as such may reveal a secret meaning expressing itself through the fragments of my own life:

The mares that carry me as far as longing can reach
rode on, once they had come and fetched me onto
the legendary road of the divinity that carries the
man who knows through the vast and dark unknown.

One of the means or methods by which Keats
could begin to equal, even exceed the inevitable
fact of decay and the equally universal and central
image of the web of life, was not to wish away the
first and imitate the second, but to try to make
himself capable of meeting, withstanding the force
of, and transforming the given of a human's
circumstance.

A vast old religion which once swayed the earth lingers
in the unbroken practice. In the oldest religion,
everything was alive, not supernaturally but naturally
alive. There were only deeper and deeper streams of
life.
For the whole life-effort of man was to get his life into
direct contact with the elemental life of the cosmos,
mountain-life, cloud-life, thunder-life, air-life,
earth-life, sun-life. To become into immediate felt
contact, and so derive energy, power and a dark sort
of joy.

The animals belong to divinities
Who come in the shape of animals
Who are animals
Saying perhaps that it is the animal in us that is holy.
Even the Kundalini is a snake
The animal that is divine is the wisdom of nature
Or the wisdom of the body
That knows from primeval times
With a knowledge which we cannot hope to emulate
No matter what we read

What we choose to fight is so tiny
What fights with us is so great
If only we would let ourselves be dominated
As things do by some immense storm
We would become strong too and not need names.

I am filled with joy
When day dawns quietly
Over the roof of the sky
Aji, jai, ja
But other times, I choke with fear;
A greedy swarm of maggots
Eats into the hollows
Of my collarbone and eyes

It is no longer enough that an occasional artist here and there should see his parcel of truth and speak it out, while the actual direction taken by civilization continues to be wholly determined by a *soi-disant*, scientific method of knowledge.

Science must itself become an art and art a science

The human soul is always moving outward into the external world and inward into itself, and this movement is double because the human soul would not be conscious were it not suspended between contraries. The greater the contrast, the more intense the consciousness.

The shadow is a tight passage, a narrow door, whose painful constriction no one is spared who goes down to the deep well. But one must learn to know oneself in order to know who one is.

For what comes after the door is, surprisingly enough, a boundless expanse full of unprecedented uncertainty, with apparently no inside and no outside, no above and no below, no here and no there.

Woman worships the male infant, not the grown man.
It is evidence of her deity, of man's dependence on her
for life. She is passionately interested in grown men,
however, because the love-hate that Osiris and Set feel
for each other on her account is a tribute to her divinity.
She tries to satisfy both, but can only do so by alternate
murder, and man tries to regard this as evidence of her
fundamental falsity, not of his own irreconcilable
demands on her.

Now let me dare to open wide the gate past
which men's steps ever flinching trod!

And while the prophets shudder or adore
Before the flame, hoping it will give ear,
If you at last must have a word to say,
Say neither, in their way,
"It is a deadly magic and accursed,
"Nor "It is blest," but only "It is here."

I feel . . . we're in a very shabby moment, and neither the literary nor the musical experience really has its finger on the pulse of our crisis. From my point of view, we're in the midst of a Flood of biblical proportions. It's both exterior and interior. At this point it's more devastating on the interior level, but it's leaking into the real world. I see everybody holding on in their individual way to an orange crate, to a piece of wood, and we're passing each other in this swollen river that has pretty well taken down all the landmarks, and pretty well overturned everything we've got.

. . . the artist has in some way or other experienced the world he represents. And in so far as his representations are appreciated, they are appreciated by those who are themselves willing to make a move towards seeing the world in that way, and, ultimately, therefore, seeing that kind of world. We should remember this, when we see pictures of a dog with six legs emerging from a vegetable marrow or a woman with a motor bicycle substituted for her left breast. Such aberrations suggest the possibility that we could very well move forward into . . . a fantastically hideous world, just as the choice to move in the direction of a further idolizing of the phenomena could move us into a world that is chaotically empty.

> Everyone would produce his or her own criteria for selecting information . . . every common norm disappears because everyone will be able to concoct his or her own interpretation of historical events (and) there won't be any common basis left on which to construct the history of the human race . . . we would end up with a society of 5,000 million inadequate memories. That's tantamount to saying that we have a society of 5,000 million languages, every one of them pidgin.

> If our social structure is disintegrating, is that not precisely because it has no constitutive spiritual principle incarnate in it?

As I now look back on these fragments of my own life, as reflected in this very incomplete and fragmented book of quotations, I do indeed begin to perceive a thread of meaning, tying my life and that of my departed friends together at last. Perhaps this perception accounts for the fact that I am no longer clear about who is exactly speaking when I speak. Which of the Three Musketeers is speaking here?

Our world is in fragments and my book of quotations itself is a collection of fragments-quotes torn from their original context over a period of many years, lying dormant until called upon for a new service—service to the unborn future. There is a mystery that draws fragments from the past together for this service. The book rearranges its pages spontaneously according to a mysterious intention to re-connect what is torn asunder, but in a new way that in effect prepares the unknown future from fragments of the past.

So many voices, singing variations of the same theme: a fragmented world, a world in which separation, isolation, breakdown may be the only norm.

With the commodification of desire that is numbing us today, I can hear the cries of anguish that arise when a being is treated as a separate fragment, unrelated to the whole, a condition that is caused by the insane proposition that the world's and our being are solely material.

The world, in which all parts are in fact related to one another is the world that has *being*. I can feel the deep longing in my book of quotations for that world, felt to be the world of the goddess. If that world is fragmented, it is not like a mechanical object being separated into parts. It is more like Marsyas being flayed—a great cry of anguish erupts. We can each find our way to this cry. We only have to refrain from withholding our attention from the fragmentation of our world. The cry will fill the seeker from below, fill his or her lungs, force the head back, open the mouth towards heaven, and escape into a wail.

Not only is there a great cry of anguish waiting for all those who have ears, but another, equally dangerous process is at work. This one is descending from above, into the material world through the vehicle of individuals who no longer know how to contain and relate to it. You could say that a fire is loose in the world, without containment.

This fire is arriving in the form of an unprecedented emergence of ideas into the material world. Inspired acts, once thought to be the exclusive province of a privileged few now are commonplace, available to increasing numbers of individuals. This fact is reflected in the unrestrained explosion of novelty in the world. Innovation was once considered by our ancestors in the light of its possible effect on culture which is conservative by nature. If the innovation was considered dangerous the author may very well have been dispatched. This is why sexuality and birth were protected by taboos. It was well understood that the new being entering the culture carried a spiritual aspect that the culture had to be careful about.

A delightful movie which illustrates this theme beautifully is *The Gods Must Be Crazy* (1980). The "new idea" is a coca cola bottle that lands in the middle of the desert in which an original people live. For the first time the people learn jealousy and conflict. The innovation is duly appraised as taboo and a warrior volunteers to send the gift back to the gods.

These taboos of course no longer hold and anything goes, to the extreme. At least one researcher, Terrence McKenna, attempted to show that the rate of which novelty is bursting into the world cannot be sustained and has an end point in time. The date of the end time given by McKenna's *Time Wave Theory* is given as December 21st, 2012—also the date that the Mayan Calendar apparently comes to an end.

While we have missed that predicted end-time and whether McKenna's *Time Wave Theory* is correct or not may not be as important for us as the fact that he noticed the fact of accelerating novelty into the world without any cultural checks and balances in place. His theory at least suggests the enormous danger of the present cascade of ideas.

Ordinary people are catapulting into fame or wealth under the impact of inspired ideas in a way that few are prepared for. All it takes is an idea, taken up by others on the basis of self-interest. The descriptions of individual encounters with the idea and of its incarnation into the world are remarkably consistent.

We are all aware of the enormous popularity of Harry Potter, for example, and of the sudden meteoric rise to fame and wealth of the author, J.K. Rowling. Her description of the process of Harry Potter's coming into being is also taken from my *Book of Quotations*:

. . . in 1990 my then boyfriend and I decided to move up to Manchester . . .it was after a weekend's flat-hunting . . . that the idea of Harry Potter simply fell into my head. I had been writing almost continuously since the age of six, but I had never been so excited about an idea before . . . all the details bubbled up in my brain, and this scrawny, black-haired bespectacled boy who didn't know he was a wizard became more and more real to me.

The phenomenon of manic-depression in the modern world is also powerful evidence for the fact that unrestrained ideas are bursting into the lives of ordinary individuals who are in no way prepared for the effects. Even a cursory glance on the Internet shows how pervasive and dangerous this syndrome is: Type in "bi-polar disorder" on a Search Engine and you get back over five million websites, many of which focus on the devastating effects that unrestrained creativity has on the lives of people. The movie on Jackson Pollock that I saw in the year 2000 is exemplary in portraying this phenomenon. A well-known book, *Touched with Fire: Manic-Depressive Illness and the Artistic Temperament*, by Kay Redfield Jamison, describes some of the effects that encountering new ideas has on individuals, and here once again I must draw from my *Book of Quotations*:

The fiery aspects of thought and feeling that initially compel the artistic voyage-fierce energy, high mood and quick intelligence; a sense of the visionary and the grand; a restless and feverish temperament – commonly carry with them the capacity for vastly darker moods, grimmer energies, and, occasionally, bouts of "madness". These opposite moods and energies, often interlaced, can appear to the world as mercurial, intemperate, volatile, brooding, troubled or stormy. In short they form the common view of the artistic temperament and, as we shall see, they also form the basis of the manic-depressive temperament.

At the moment we are in huge cultural conflict concerning the emergence of new ideas. On the one hand science holds up its unassailable "prime directive": the pursuit of knowledge must be completely free of interference! On the other hand organized religion and political movements are raising their voice against the proliferation of untested ideas making their way into our lives, through the agency of technology.

My work, and the work of my friends, as it speaks through me now, is based on the proposition that this fragmentation in our lives and in the world *means something*, as paradoxical as that must sound!

As my friend Gary once put it, we are moving from fragments to fractal and it was Po' who then drew my attention to my collection of quotations, suggesting that a fractal is beginning to emerge from within those fragments, or shards, as I later came to call them. She then enigmatically proposed that those of us who take up this task are in effect *preparing the unknown future*. How so, I asked? As she so often did, Po' refused this grasping after explanation. It bored her. So I had to wait and incubate the question, just as she had taught us all the practice of *phōlarchos*, so long ago. Finally the answer came and it came of course in the form of yet two more shards that found their way into my *Book of Quotations.*

Let us imagine that different futures are possible from the same past and that it takes only a minor variation to lead to a profound bifurcation with the past and that the source of that "minor variation" is pictured to us in those experiences we call dreams, particularly big dreams. So it would be what we "construct" with the guidance of the big dream, how we enact the big dream that will yield a rich new way of leading us into the future.

Man looks out over the chimneys, the factories, the telephones —everything that technology has produced in wondrous ways in the most recent times. He stands atop this purely mechanical world, the grave of all things spiritual, and he calls out longingly into the universe—and his yearning will be fulfilled. Just as the dead stone yields the living fiery spark if handled correctly, so from our dead technology will emerge the living spirit, if human beings have the right feelings about what technology is.

It began to dawn on me that Gary and Po' were pointing to the idea that fragments are not only the shards of a destroyed totality, the world of the goddess. Yes, there is unspeakable grief deep within each of us regarding this irrecoverable loss. Yet, at the same time, each shard also carries a *possible future* within it.

How can this be?

This question has become the preoccupation of my remaining years. I have curled up in my lair and fallen into the same hypnogogic state that Edgar knew so well. But which Edgar am I talking about? I seem to remember four or five Edgars. I remember the brain researcher in *this* life alright but there were, are (?) several others, one of which is the master of the hypnogogic state. Are they less real than *this* one? From this, what shall I call it, time-line, they appear to me as fragments: of dreams, or even memories, but they also carry a feeling of independent lives, lived *somewhere else.* Bits and pieces of these complete lives break through into *this* space, and we call them dreams or memories. These shards then began to work on me, altering my life in concrete ways, and in so doing, they came more into focus in *this* life, which I now hesitate to call *mine.*

It's more like Edgar, Gary, Allen, and Po' are coming to life *through* my life here, becoming my actual future and at the same time, entering *this* world.

Just now, right now, as I write this last sentence down, I can hear Po' speak: Yes, John, all good so far. But you must emphasize the path! How can we reach the "place" where possible futures can reach us? What do we need to do? Remember, John, remember Gary. It was his death that taught us. Edgar gave us a hint with *his* death, but it was Gary who shows us the way.

Gary, John!

2011: GARY'S DEATH

"Unless your past perishes," Sophia said to me, "you are doomed. Do you know that?"

Philip K. Dick

GARY LAY THERE QUIETLY. HE was dying. And he knew
it. All resistance was gone now. His exposed brain was
thoroughly infected with the bacteria that had rapidly
invaded through his nose, once the meninges had broken down.

He "knew" it was coming, he had been warned after all.
It's just that dreams emerge from a reality that does not easily
translate into predictions in this, our ordinary reality. The
meaning can go in many directions at once. These dreams
however had a particular emphasis on "physicality", and death.
Gary had felt alarmed upon awakening. With good reason, as it
turned out! He had dreamed:

> I notice my right leg. It is almost eaten away around the
> bone which is quite exposed. Flesh is hanging off. It has
> obviously been this way for some time. Well, there is
> no going for work now. That is over! I am under a tree
> and a dog comes, sniffing. He goes for my leg. At first I
> am alarmed then realize it is only food for him. A horse
> comes by. Now, some people come. They are from the
> organisation that assists with the passage across. I am
> relieved and I start weeping. Memories come and I finally
> remember my son Chris, I wish he were here, but not to
> be. I see a skull. It is mine but how can that be? As I turn it

> slowly in my hands I marvel at how at one time my brain
> was in there. Now the time is close I feel my breath going
> and I ask to be taken under the willow tree to go quietly.

And then the second dream:

> I decide to kill myself. A bullet in the head, but it does not
> kill me only knocks out brain functions. So now I am alive
> but in a very different way. I see Viv, (who killed himself)
> who tells me that meningitis is next. I move into a flat
> in an inner city area, almost slum, where I will become
> the "Sage of Underwood" or some such. Kate, the actress
> from Underbelly, sings nearby to me and the song is
> beautiful; just beautiful.

When Gary gathered himself enough to reflect, he noticed the definite emphasis of the dreams on the brain and its demise. He also had learned from Po' that dreams are fragments of *possible futures*, not merely reflections of the past. That helped Gary make sense of the dream fact that he had a son, Chris, even though in this life he had never married and had no children. Po' had also told him that it therefore makes a huge difference how we participate in those movements emerging out of the forming future.

Gary was familiar enough, thanks to his collaboration with Edgar, with current advances in neuroscience to know that modern consciousness exists only as inextricably linked with the brain and the central nervous system. Some researchers go as far as claiming to predict what we think by simply looking at a MRI scan and observing the section of the brain that "lights up"! Gary's dreams with their focus on the brain's demise could therefore be addressing a death of that *brain-linked* consciousness, a death that must be undergone! And death is final!

Yet both dreams pointed also to a form of *existence* in which the link between consciousness and the brain is severed. The first dream showed Gary contemplating his own skull, the skull that once housed his brain. The second dream explicitly described him as being "alive but in a very different way".

Gary then remembered an article he had once read in TIME magazine, and he had learned from Allen and Po' not to ignore such sudden intrusions into consciousness of these seemingly disconnected fragments of meaning. They had taught him to follow up on the hint, *without* knowing, i.e., without the benefit of brain-based consciousness—a task that Gary had found extremely difficult at first.

The TIME issue was devoted to current research exploring the ties consciousness has to the brain with the predominant conclusion that without the brain, consciousness ceases to exist. The particular article that Gary now remembered was a counter-example to the prevailing wisdom. The author is an orthopedic surgeon who describes a patient whose brain "had already been destroyed" and yet woke up to say goodbye coherently to his family.

My god, Gary thought, that is what happened to Edgar, too!

He was next drawn to the disturbing image of meningitis appearing in the dream as an ominous sense of what was to come "next". Meningitis is a disease in which bacteria or virus invades the meninges, the membranes that cover and protect the brain tissue. There are three layers: the *pita mater*, *arachnoid mater*, and *dura mater*—tender mother, spider mother, and hard mother. Gary was jolted when he read this description.

My entire brain, my thinking depends on and is protected by these three aspects of the mother. What does this mean? Gary could now feel the presence of one who he loved—Po'!

"Keep going," she whispered. "You are close to something."

Does this mean that the Mother supports and protects our present brain-based consciousness, reflective knowledge, i.e., knowledge gained by a consciousness that is separate from everything else and is always "of the past" because reflective?

What a strange and compelling thought!

This, our reflective knowledge is static, petrified, frozen, not living, yet the Mother lies behind it and supports it. Wait a minute, and now Gary's mind was rushing like rapids. Of course, petrifaction and reflection irresistibly invoke the image of the gorgon, Medusa. It is she, who, like the triune meninges of my dream, lies behind all such knowledge and its petrifying effect on living process.

Then an even stranger thought forced its way in. Gary thought he heard a peal of laughter, or is it distant bells, no, a whale song, coming up from the depths?

What happens, as he thought his way carefully into the living thinking that was now upon him, what happens if she withdraws her support, and the petrified stone shatters?

We get *shards*, that's what happens! And we die! We *must* die, first and foremost.

A shard floated in front of his mind.

Good heavens, he thought, I read that in Allen's collection of quotations, what did he call them, fragments, in an old shoe box. He showed us that box once, when he was kicked out the Academy.

Wait a minute! Allen was never in the Academy. Far from it, he became something of a polymath, but he eschewed all institutions. But I have this distinct memory . . .

Gary's meninges were now no longer protecting his brain-based consciousness and he was being released to his death. The connection between the knowledge gained by this form of consciousness and the mother whose petrifying stare reduces all living processes to stone lingered with him as he lay quietly in his bed. He began to remember episodes from his own past. He allowed the images to parade before him, as friends might come by for a visit to the departing one. They were shards, fragments, seemingly no longer held together in a contrived continuity by a self-edifying ego. They came in whatever order, or disorder . . .

As they arrived, first in a trickle, Gary found that he could "ride" one, if he chose, on the basis of attraction or aversion. When that happened, his present state of dying, under the tree where he had been placed, retreated as if receding down a long tunnel and he would become the memory, reliving its feeling, its consciousness.

And so he "woke up" in a class room:

"No! You are wrong! You are all wrong! The forces acting on that object sliding down the inclined plane resolve into these partial forces, not those! I'll prove it to you. I am going to send the entire problem to someone at the University of Queensland and we'll see what he says."

Laughter, Mocking.

"Einstein!"

"Dear Gary, thank you for sending me this problem on mechanical forces. As you can see from my diagram, your construction is not quite right. The forces rather resolve this way when we place the co-ordinate system on the inclined plane . . . Yours sincerely, Dr . . ."

Humiliation!

Michael McMullan. Fat—the butt of many jokes, always trying to belong. I treated him badly. I really wanted to be friends. Why doesn't he come over to my place? I always go to his. He wants to be with Wayne Goldstein who always rubbishes him, sparing no pains to humiliate him publically . . .

University of Queensland! I love this place. Physics, Maths, conversations, arguments, study!

"Michael, I bet you don't know . . ."

"Well Gary, my man, all that depends on truth. What is truth, my man?"

Silence.

My god, he knows something I do not. He protects himself against the "Goldstein attacks" with knowledge. He must be studying philosophy. Now I can see how to protect myself against humiliation. I won't be caught off guard again. For starters, I am going to learn a word every day from the dictionary. And, I am going to strengthen my stomach muscles. You can never tell when someone might come at you with a good kick . . .

The shard drifted away and Gary looked up at the overarching branches of the willow tree that sheltered him in his last moments.

So that is what I was doing—for so long protecting myself with a carefully constructed edifice of knowledge. Protecting myself from what? Humiliation, mockery, maybe terror! At whose hands? Who stands behind this edifice of knowledge? I have pursued this kind of knowledge for decades, drawing not only from my personal past but the deep past as well.

Gary then recalled a dream fragment. "You are a Knight Templar," it simply said.

He caught hold of this particular shard and remembered the excitement he had felt when he learned that the vows that the Knight took were: *Poverty, Chastity, and Obedience.*

These are my vows! How I lived them during my life!

Memories of being drawn to junk, cast-off clothes, left-over foods, looking for money in the gutters, dreaming of wealth acquired through finding the 1932 penny that was so rare; strangely shy and modest in all things sexual; first girlfriend as late bloomer while at the University of Queensland; eager to obey authority . . . Just tell me what to do!

More shards arrived.

Our past goes further back than the 14th C.

Gary had engaged with Allen in vigorous discussions of the theory of evolution and its geologic time, finally aligning himself with those who understood evolution as a simultaneous evolution of consciousness and world. He came to understand that present day consciousness was simply an outcome and a transformation of former states of consciousness and their correlative world. For example, he marveled at the paintings found in the caves of Southern France, at Lascaux, over 30 000 years old.

What form of consciousness did we have then?

Gary could feel the old excitement as he recalled the years of study he had given over to the study of the evolution of consciousness and the world, focusing on what happens to the world when consciousness undergoes a transformation. His specialty lay in the field of chaos theory and, with his friends' help, had successfully linked his studies with those of consciousness studies. In particular he had been gripped by the image of the vortex and its unique features in the phenomenon of turbulence. And hadn't the four friends, what did Allen call us, the Three Musketeers, and Constance of course, for some mad reason, entered the vortex when they were so young? Or was it a dream? Whatever it was, it was real and life-changing . . .

Now the memories did not have quite such a grip on him. They gathered around his bed under the old willow tree but their hold on him was tenuous at best.

He began to realize that these memories were indeed shards. Any meaning they each had was an invested one by a brain-based consciousness that *needed to know*. This must be why we are constantly revising our history texts, our theories of evolution etc. Why, we even revise our personal histories under the influence of therapy or education.

Gary realized that the meaning-making factor must lie within us! When we take up any shard, be it personal or geological, any meaning we "find" must have arisen from within us in the first place. So, deep within our almost obsessive preoccupation with the past and within the myriad self-serving interpretations of the past, must be an impulse to come to know the being from which we emerged in the form of our modern day consciousness. Usually a culture favors one interpretation or another and this passes as the "truth". But really this truth is nothing more than an official narrative that serves that culture's need to explain its own origin.

A much more interesting question arose for Gary. What happens when an individual understands this curious "manufacturing" of knowledge of the past? What happens if this individual no longer wishes to favor *any* interpretation of the past?

"Let the shards remain shards!" He heard Po' shout with joy! "Yes, Gary, show us the way!"

No sooner had these words left Gary's mouth when a gentle breeze sprung up and began to move the willow branches softly. Like so many leaves, the shards of memories that had gathered around him, as he lay there dying began to tremble and whirl.

As the late afternoon sun broke through the thick canopy, it seemed to resolve itself into a form. Gary saw a pair of wings folded forward and eyes that were staring backwards as the light-being, for that surely what it was, began to surge backwards. Its unearthly eyes were fixed on the shards that were gathered there, drawing them together in what became a torrent of glittering light fragments, likewise surging backwards so that angel and shards were moving ever apart, with an increasing velocity, yet the whole scene danced motionless before Gary's eyes. He heard a dull roar as this catastrophe gained momentum. The angel, moving ever towards the future backwards had its eyes fixed unwaveringly on the shards of the past as its thundering wings beat the torrent into a frothing ever-departing storm wave. The roar became a cacophony in Gary's ear and the light gathered in intensity until all he could see was a blinding river of shattered light forms. His last thought was:

Allen, you told me about this. You told me about Walter's vision of the angel of history. It's true, Allen! Can you hear me, it's true! It's the UR-image!

And then, Gary died.

2013: THE VOICE OF PO'

[W]hat is the spiral necessity at the innermost geography of hearing?

Russell Lockhart

GARY HAS PASSED AND EDGAR has been dead for some years now. Po' has disappeared and I believe Allen is still alive, somewhere.

What remains?

A breeze starts up and shakes a willow tree. Leaves break off easily as it is now autumn. Each leaf tumbles down softly to the ground. Some are trampled on by passers-by. Some decay quite naturally. Others are blown away to god knows where.

I know this is where Gary really died, although he died in hospital like most of us will. I bend down to pick up a reddish-brown leaf, red like the setting sun. I briefly look up into that sun, lying low on the horizon. A long dusty road stretches out before me. A small dust-devil springs up swirling the Australian red dirt into a spiral. Four shapes form briefly in silhouette and then, as the sun sets finally, the vision collapses.

As I casually pick up four more leaves I notice out of the corner of my eye that a dingo is watching me from the road side, quite unafraid, almost curious about what I will do next. I straighten up and he turns, melting silently into the darkening Australian bush.

I glance down into my hand and find five poems, written on some scraps of old faded paper. I look up sharply as I hear a golden laugh, joyous, fading into the distance like the red Australian sun.

Or is it bells, or a whale, sounding from immense depths?

SOUL BIRD

effortless winged flight
where you pass
day becomes night

some gaze in
ready to die

black hole in the sky
rent by your eerie cry

fewer take wing
plunge down through the wound

many glance up
feet safe on the ground

that you may be heard
where cry becomes word

WRIT UPON

impassive cursive stroking
skin welting seering
ineluctable inscripting
terror'd body arching
vellum heart writ upon

graceful head inclining
gentle hand pausing
angel listening . . . eternal
book softly closing
inevitable

death's hand steadying
open mouth contorting
wrenching into soundwording
still'd at last

final . . .

end

DEATH'S WILL

heart still'd

death's will

terror'd heart

                    now depart

still'd lake

now awake

EDGE

at the edge

everything is dead . . .

infinite deepening

wave weeping in

dead thing seeking

if you want to live

go to the shore

become a corpse

FOREST

you are only lost

when you know

where you are going

surrender your certainty

death will show the way

ABOUT THE AUTHOR

J OHN C. WOODCOCK HOLDS A doctorate in Consciousness Studies (1999). His thesis articulates the process and outcome of a spiritual ordeal that lasted twenty years. At first it seemed to John that he was undergoing a purely personal psychological crisis but over time, with assistance from his various mentors, he discovered that he was also participating in the historical process of a transformation of the soul as reflected in the enormous changes occurring in our culture, often referred to as apocalyptic. During this difficult period of John's life, he wrote two books: *Living in Uncertainty* and *Making of a Man.* Both books have been expanded into second editions (2012).

Over time John began to comprehend how our modern reality, seemingly so bereft of soul, is indeed itself a manifestation of soul. Soul and world were found to be a unity of differences. This discovery opened up the possibility of discerning soul movement from within present external reality, comprising hints of the possible futures. John's next three books, *The Coming Guest, The Imperative,* and *Hearing Voices,* explore this idea more fully by describing the initiatory process and outcome of one individual's becoming a vehicle for the expression of the unknown future, through the medium of his or her art. John's latest book, *Animal Soul,* establishes a firm theoretical ground for the claim that the soul is urging us towards the development of new inner capacities that together he calls the augur-artist mind—the mind that can discern and artistically render hints of possible futures. In this new book John gives a more refined definition of the genre of literature that can adequately express/describe a new reality that is forming in the unconscious—one that overcomes the oppositions that characterize the Cartesian reality principle.

John currently lives with his wife Anita in Sydney, where he teaches, writes, and consults with others concerning their soul life. He is also a practicing Jungian therapist.

He may be contacted at *jwoodcock@lighthousedownunder.com.*